"What's your role in this operation?"

A negotiation. Isin could play this game with his eyes closed. "I'm captain of *Vengeance*. A mercenary warship."

"They provide muscle when needed." Natasha shot him another warning look. "I'm captain of *Phoenix*. The passenger freighter I mentioned."

Green glanced between them, assessing. "I see."

"We can split up the cargo between the two ships if necessary, depending on what you need transported."

Green pinned Isin with a hard stare. "How many on your crew?"

"Twenty-one."

"All mercenaries?"

"Except for my medic."

"And is your crew loyal? Trustworthy?"

Isin met her stare for stare. "As long as they get paid."

Green's lips pursed, her gaze shifting to Natasha. "And what about your crew?"

"Definitely trustworthy. We're not mercenaries. We're freight runners."

The silent condemnation in her tone loosened Isin's tongue. "And smugglers and thieves."

Natasha kicked his leg with the heel of her boot. "Only if the job requires it."

MARKED MERCENARIES

Starhawke Rogue Book Two

Audrey Sharpe

Ocean Dance Press

MARKED MERCENARIES
© 2019 Audrey Sharpe

ISBN: 978-1-946759-75-7

Ocean Dance Press, LLC
PO Box 69901
Oro Valley AZ 85737

Cover art by Significant Cover

Visit the author's website at:
AudreySharpe.com

One

Natasha Orlov was going to kill him.

Elhadj Isin watched her from the corner of his eye as she entered the crew gym on *Phoenix's* A deck. He continued his reps with the barbell, but every molecule in his body vibrated with tension.

She wouldn't do it intentionally, of course. Natasha was many things—a pilot, a smuggler, a beautiful pain-in-the-ass. But a cold-blooded killer? Never.

That particular label only applied to him. Or at least it had. When she'd blasted back into his life with a sharp-tongued retort and a kick to his solar plexus, she'd dislodged the permanent iceberg in his chest. Now it bobbed through his veins like a grenade with a loose pin. He hadn't figured out what to do about it.

She stopped just inside the gym's entrance, her gaze sweeping the room and settling on him. A frown pulled down the corners of her lips as she stared at the scars on his face and bare chest. The look in her pale aqua eyes no longer held the abject horror she'd shown the first time she'd seen the evidence of his brutal past, but her expression was hardly complimentary.

He didn't want to take it personally. Her discomfort at seeing the scars crisscrossing his skin shouldn't bother him.

It did. Especially since she was the reason he'd encouraged the wounds in the first place.

He tracked her as she made her way across the room like a heat-seeking missile, stopping at the foot of the weight bench.

"We need to talk."

His least favorite way to start a conversation. "Go ahead." He'd already completed his normal set of reps for the day, but he kept lifting the barbell in a fluid motion. Whatever she had to say would be easier to hear if he didn't have to gaze into her eyes while she said it.

"We'll be at Gallows Edge in a few hours. I want to clarify how this deal of yours is going to work so we prevent any… misunderstandings."

He might have laughed if he wasn't fighting to keep his breathing steady while his muscles strained against the extra reps. Natasha had a gift for understatement. *Misunderstandings* was code for lying, deceit, and betrayal. "What do you want to know?"

"For one thing, you've indicated *Vengeance* has about twenty crewmembers. I have Pete, Marlin, and myself. If you're planning to send your entire crew out on the job hunt, that's hardly a level playing field."

"Um-hmm." He couldn't shrug while holding the barbell, but he managed to convey the idea with a glance.

Natasha growled and fisted her hands on her lean hips. She looked like an angry sprite. "*Are* you planning to send your entire crew?"

"I hadn't decided yet."

Her expression darkened, just as he'd intended.

He shouldn't enjoy taunting her. But the fire that sparked in her eyes when she got riled up fascinated him. As did her courage. Physically he could dominate her with one hand tied behind his back, but she always held her ground against him, refusing to be cowed, even when she believed he meant her harm.

As if he would ever lay a finger on her. He owed her his life. As long as he drew breath, no one would harm a single hair on her head.

Maybe on some level she sensed that. Or maybe she believed some shred of the man she'd once known still existed under his battered exterior.

She was wrong. After she'd risked her life to save him from the Setarips on Troi, he'd destroyed that weak, pathetic version of himself—a fitting punishment for his cowardice and incompetence. But Natasha's distaste for the man he'd become didn't sit well.

"Isin..." Natasha's jaw clenched as she gritted her teeth.

He lowered the barbell to his chest, a slight tremor in his upper arms warning him that he'd have to give in to his body's demands soon. But not yet. He forced the heavy load back up. "I'll only bring Itorye." His first mate had a gift for finding wealthy employers. Itorye had grown up in a privileged family, just as he had. She understood how the game was played, and didn't hesitate to use her beauty and charm to best advantage.

"I have your word on that?"

He met Natasha's gaze. "Does that matter? The word of a mercenary?" She'd been taking jabs at him regarding his chosen profession ever since they'd been reunited.

Her throat moved in a convulsive swallow, but she didn't look away. "It does to me."

Why, oh why, did that warm his heart? He shouldn't care whether she saw him as an honorable man. But he did. He was a fool. "You have my word." He'd proposed this wager, and she deserved a chance to win, even if he had every intention of making sure she didn't.

Her chin dipped in a small nod. But rather than leaving, she continued to study him.

Now *he* was the one feeling uncomfortable. And exhausted. When he tried to push the barbell away from his chest, his muscles screamed in protest.

He was *not* going to ask for her help. He'd gotten himself into this mess by not pausing when she'd arrived. He'd get himself out. With a Herculean effort, he forced the barbell up until he could drop it into the cradle. It clanged loud enough to echo in the close confines of the room.

Keeping his breathing steady was a challenge with his heart pounding like a freight train, but he managed. He'd spent the past year learning to conceal any sign of physical discomfort or weakness. "Was there something else?"

"What are your plans after we arrive?"

He sat up, putting him at eye level with her. She was so petite that when he was standing, the top of her head barely reached his shoulder. "I'll check on *Vengeance.*" He hadn't been on his ship in weeks. Itorye had kept the crew busy during the unexpected hiatus, completing all the routine maintenance as well as most of the long-overdue repairs. The ship would be in tiptop condition.

"So you won't be leaving the docks right away?"

The speculative look in her eyes told him exactly what she was thinking. He gave her a hard stare. "No. And if you want to keep the playing field level, you'll wait on *Phoenix* until I'm done."

Her gaze shifted to the scars on his chest, her lips pressing into a line. "I can do that."

He had the irrational urge to grab his tunic and pull it on. He didn't.

"Do you know where you'll be heading?" she asked, folding her arms.

"You expect me to tell you?"

She shrugged. "Why not? I won't follow you."

Her nonchalance set off alarm bells. Given her history, *he* might be wise to follow *her.* He'd only been to Gallows Edge once, shortly after he'd signed on with *Vengeance.* At the time his mood had been so black he honestly didn't remember much about the place, except that it spelled trouble with a capital T. "Where are *you* heading after we dock?"

"The lower levels."

So she did have a plan. "Anywhere in particular?"

"Doohan's Bar."

He'd never heard of it. But she obviously had. "You've been there before?"

A flash of pain bloomed in her pale eyes, which she quickly squelched. "Yes."

There was a lot more to the story. But her body language told him pushing for information would be futile. "And you think you'll be able to pick up a lucrative freight job there?"

"I might."

He didn't buy her casual tone for a moment. If she was willing to share her plan, she had an *excellent* chance of finding a client at Doohan's Bar.

He *really* might want to consider following her. She'd specified Gallows Edge as the location for this competition for a reason. He'd underestimated her resourcefulness. Again.

"Maybe I'll join you."

Her eyes widened a fraction. "Why?"

"A bar's a good place to find mercenary work." Not the kind of work he preferred, but in this case, he'd take anything that paid the agreed upon minimum to win the bet. "Is that a problem?"

She was too much of a professional liar to give any kind of tell, but he knew she wasn't happy. "Not at all. I'll arrange transportation." She glanced over her shoulder. "I should get back to the bridge." With a slight lift to her chin, she pivoted on her heel and strode out of the room.

He stared after her. *What was she hiding?*

Two

"Coming out of the jump now." Natasha eased the ship through the transition from interstellar to main engines with the seamless grace of a swan gliding through water.

Isin checked the tactical display, which showed the distant sun and orbiting planets of the system that housed Gallows Edge. No sign of *Vengeance*, yet. But they wouldn't be far behind. "Hold position."

Natasha shot him a look, but the ship's forward momentum slowed. "We can wait for them, but when we reach the moon, we'll need to dock first." Her tone left no room for argument.

So he argued. "Why? Afraid I won't keep my word?"

"That has nothing to do with it."

"Then why?"

She met his gaze. "You'll understand when we get there."

"Why don't you explain now?" He pivoted his chair to face her and crossed his arms over his chest. "We have time."

Her jaw worked, as if she were chewing her words to make them easier to digest. "Let's just say that I get special treatment at Gallows Edge."

An unpleasant prickle spread over his skin. "What kind of special treatment?"

"Expedited docking privileges."

"I see." Her attitude puzzled him. She had the pinched look she got whenever she was facing something unpleasant, and yet she'd picked this location. Why would she insist they come here if she didn't like....

An awful idea popped into his head. "Are you setting me up?"

"Setting you up?"

"Staging an ambush for me and my crew so you can take the *Phoenix*?"

She stared at him like he'd lost his mind. "An ambush?" The corners of her mouth started to twitch, a muffled snort escaping between her compressed lips.

"Is that amusing?"

Her grin broke through, quickly turning into a full-blown belly laugh, her body shaking like he'd said the funniest thing she'd heard in years.

Too bad he wasn't in on the joke. "Are you finished?"

She covered her mouth with her hand, her laughter fading. "Yeah. But thanks for that." Her gaze returned to the bridgescreen as she shook her head and murmured something that sounded like *paranoid mercenary*. "And to answer your question, no, I haven't planned an ambush."

"Then why do you look anxious to be here?"

All mirth drained from her expression, taking her vitality with it. "Simple. Tnaryt? The Setarip who captured me? He used this system as his home base."

That explained the dread. "If it has bad memories, why are we here?" She could have picked any location she wanted. She'd chosen this one.

"Because I can get us free food and supplies." She glanced at him out of the corner of her eye. "A *lot* of free food and supplies."

Now it was his turn to stare. "How?"

She shrugged. "The outpost admins believed Tnaryt would attack and destroy them if they didn't provide whatever he wanted. The arrangement was already in place when I came on the scene. He had me take over the shuttle run duty from the Setarip pilot."

"But you said Tnaryt's dead."

"No one on Gallows Edge knows that. The ship went down in another system. As far as the admins are concerned, his ship's still out there, and he'll attack if they fail to deliver his shipment."

Her reasons for choosing this location were coming into focus. "But you've been gone a while. Won't they find it suspicious that he hasn't sent anyone to pick up his supplies recently?"

"No. He never had a pattern. Sometimes he'd send me out once or twice a week. Other times once or twice a month. Depended on his mood. And if they believe he's been off pillaging or fighting the other Setarip factions...."

He caught her line of reasoning. "They won't think anything's amiss. Especially if you show up with two ships that could be spoils of war."

She nodded. "Exactly."

"Except we won't have any Setarips with us."

"I never did before, either. As far as I could tell, the only Setarip they ever saw in person was the original pilot, and he stopped going with me after the first run we made together."

"So the admins believe you have a direct line to Tnaryt?"

"That's right."

"And as long as you lead us in, they'll assume we're all working for the Setarips."

"Yes, they should." The lines of tension on her face deepened. "If they discover the Setarip threat has been eliminated, things could get... dicey."

That possibility didn't worry him half as much as her potential connections on Gallows Edge. She had a definite advantage here. Or maybe not. She certainly couldn't ask the admins to find her a freight job. That wouldn't jibe with her cover story as a servant for the Setarips. But she might know other people here, perhaps someone she planned to meet at the bar she'd mentioned. "These supplies... how much food are we talking about?"

"Enough to feed our crews for a couple months."

A couple months?

She glanced at him, a tiny smile creasing her cheek. "I figure we can add that amount to the income total for whatever job I land."

Two months worth of free supplies was a heck of a bonus. And pushed him even further into a corner. "Hmm." This development would make winning their bet more complicated.

Not that it had ever been simple. And if she landed a freight run before he and Itorye secured a mercenary job, he'd have to convince his crew to serve as cargo couriers under Natasha's command for the duration of the delivery. Or face a mutiny. The free supplies might smooth some ruffled feathers, but keeping the crew of trigger-happy fighters under control was challenging even when they were doing the work they'd signed on for. After the recent downtime, they'd be itching for action.

But he was the idiot who'd come up with this brilliant wager. He'd have to see it through.

"*Vengeance* just entered the system," Natasha informed him.

He glanced at the visual display. The warship was approaching on their starboard side, its heavily armored prow making it look like a charging rhinoceros. He opened a comm channel. "Isin to Itorye."

"Yes?"

"Natasha will be leading us to the docks. Follow her in and do not respond to any hails until you hear from me."

If Itorye was surprised by the order, she didn't indicate it. "Understood."

"I'll meet you on *Vengeance* after we dock."

Itorye didn't miss a beat. "Aye."

He closed the channel and focused his attention on the bridgescreen as Natasha guided the *Phoenix* toward the planet that anchored Gallows Edge in the system. The thick cloud layer concealed the planet's uninhabitable surface, but the mineral resources on the moons had provided a decade of mining operations before the ore had run out and the mines had shut down.

From what he'd heard, special interests had purchased the abandoned facility, converting it into a privately run outpost for travelers and merchants in this sector of the galaxy. Gallows Edge's isolated position in the outer rim, and its proximity to Teeli space, made it a perfect location for black market dealings of all kinds. The Galactic Fleet rarely passed this way. No wonder the Setarips had claimed dominion here.

A light on the comm console flashed and a chime sounded. Natasha opened the channel for the incoming hail.

"Unidentified vessel. What is your business here?" The words were innocuous enough, but a thinly veiled warning came with it.

Natasha shot Isin a look, touching a finger to her lips before facing the comm camera and turning on the video feed.

He stared, fascinated by the abrupt change in her demeanor. The irreverent and spunky woman he knew had been replaced by a stoic ice queen.

"Hello, Cutler."

The dark-haired man on the video monitor paled, his eyes widening. "P-Pilot. I'm s-sorry. I didn't know it was you."

"Clearly." Natasha's tone contained zero inflection, but she still managed to convey displeasure and a subtle threat.

Cutler rushed to fill the silence. "W-We haven't seen you in a while. We d-didn't know you were c-coming—"

Natasha slashed a hand through the air, silencing any further protestations. "We have two vessels to dock, *Phoenix* and *Vengeance.* I want adjacent berths cleared in Alpha section."

"R-Right away."

Natasha gazed into the camera, unblinking, like an owl watching an unsuspecting mouse. "I'm transmitting a supply list now. I trust it will be ready within the hour?"

Cutler's skin went from pale to grey. His gaze darted to the side, triggering a flurry of movement behind him. "O-Of course. We'll have everything waiting."

Natasha acknowledged him with the barest tilt of her head before shutting off the feed. Her shoulders slumped and her head drooped as she closed her eyes.

Her performance had been flawless. And chilling. He'd just witnessed who she'd become while she was with the Setarips. What had Tnaryt done to her to elicit such a change? How badly did those memories haunt her?

He drew in a slow breath, unclenching his fists. Too bad the bastard was already dead. He would have enjoyed facing off against the Setarip in *Vengeance's* fight cage.

And slowly bleeding the life out of him. "That was interesting."

Her eyelids lifted like they had weights attached to them. She met his gaze. "And it will only work once. We'll have to make it count."

Three

As soon as Natasha settled *Phoenix* in the docking berth, Isin headed for the cabin he'd shared with Kenji and Shash during their stay onboard.

When they'd first encountered Natasha and her crew on the sand dunes of Troi, he'd kept a close eye on his gunner and engineer to make sure they wouldn't do something stupid, like hurt Natasha. Especially Shash. She'd hated Natasha on sight. And Shash had a hard time playing nice with those she disliked.

But the danger had passed more quickly than he'd anticipated. Kenji seemed genuinely fond of the *Phoenix* crew, especially Marlin, and while Shash's antipathy hadn't diminished, she hadn't given any sign of acting on it, either.

Their voices drifted out of the cabin as he strode down the A deck passageway.

"...can't wait to leave this rattletrap." Shash's voice, sounding unusually disgruntled.

"Ha! Save your breath." A chuckle followed Kenji's reply. "I saw how you acted when you were working with Stevens in the engine room. You like this ship, and you know it."

"No I don't! It's—"

"It's what?" Isin asked, leaning his shoulder against the doorjamb.

Shash's lips pursed. She shot a glare at Kenji before facing Isin. "It's not *Vengeance*."

"No, it's not." And Shash loved *Vengeance* like a mother loves her child. But he agreed with Kenji. Shash had developed an attachment to *Phoenix*, too. "And I want you back on *Vengeance.* Inspect all the ship's systems and run diagnostics on the repair and maintenance work Itorye had the crew do while we were gone. No one's off duty until everything meets with your approval."

Shash's dark eyes glittered. Running the crew ragged was one of her favorite tasks. "No problem."

Kenji slung his bag over his shoulder. "Does that include me?"

Isin shook his head. "I need you to acquire weapons upgrades for *Phoenix.* We'll be taking her into more dangerous situations than she was designed to handle. She'll need better defenses."

Kenji looked as pleased with his assignment as Shash. "You've got it."

"One other thing. The authorities here believe we're working for a faction of Setarips. That's why I'm wearing this." He pulled down the collar of his tunic to reveal a circle of metal Natasha had given him to wear before he'd left the bridge.

Kenji frowned. "What is that?"

"A facsimile of a control collar, like the one Natasha wore when she was a captive." Saying the words made his jaw clench. He pushed the unpleasant image from his mind. "She and I will both be wearing them."

"Why?"

"Because the authorities don't know the Setarips are dead. And Natasha can get us two months of free supplies if we follow her lead."

Kenji whistled. "That's worth a bit of acting."

"Agreed. After the supplies are delivered, all crewmembers except you, Itorye, and myself are to remain onboard *Vengeance.* No exceptions." They couldn't afford any mistakes.

"What if someone on the outpost starts asking me questions about the weapons purchases?"

"Don't answer them. And if they give you a hard time, tell them to take it up with the Setarip pilot. That should shut them down." It had certainly worked with the port authorities.

Shash made a face. "What if Orlov blows our cover?"

Isin straightened. He didn't like her tone one bit. "She won't." Natasha had as much riding on this as they did. Maybe more. He took a step forward. "And neither will you. If she gives you an order, you follow it. No arguments. Do we understand each other?"

Resentment shone in her eyes, but it wasn't directed at him. "Yeah."

"Good. I'll meet you in the bay."

Shash stuffed her remaining belongings in her pack and stalked out of the room, but Kenji waited while Isin gathered the few possessions he'd brought with him from *Vengeance.*

Kenji's gaze drifted to the doorway. "She may like this ship, but she purely hates Orlov."

"I know." Shash had done everything in her power to not share the same space as Natasha during the weeks of repairs to *Phoenix* and the two-day journey to Gallows Edge. "Which is why they won't be working together." *Phoenix* already had a talented engineer—Pete Stevens. Shash was redundant. And she and Natasha would both be happier on separate ships.

Kenji walked beside him as they descended the stairs to the bay. *Gypsy,* Natasha's shuttle, sat in the center of the open space, fully repaired after the tumultuous flight that had damaged the shuttle during their battle with the Feds on Troi.

Shash stood off to one side, while Natasha had taken up her post at the top of the bay's loading ramp, her arms folded and her gaze focused on the section of the dock visible through the open bay doors. She glanced over her shoulder as they approached. Her expression matched the ice queen persona she'd exhibited during the video chat with the tower.

"Any problems?" he murmured as he stopped beside her.

"No." The duster that surrounded her petite form, combined with the firm set of her jaw, made her a formidable figure despite her petite stature. A slight bulge in the fabric of her turtleneck was all he could see of her collar. He hadn't even noticed she'd been wearing it during the flight in until she'd produced the one she'd made for him and laid out her plan. "They just arrived with the first load of supplies." She indicated a cadre of workers hurrying to unload crates from a large cargo transport. "I told them to deliver this set to *Phoenix*, then take the rest to *Vengeance*."

"Do you need help supervising here?" He didn't like the idea of leaving her alone, even if *Vengeance* was just in the next berth.

"No." She glanced at his neck, where the faux collar sat against his skin, and gave him a small nod of approval. "We'll follow the plan. Make sure you keep crew interaction with the workers to a minimum. I'll notify you when I'm ready to leave the docks."

He couldn't argue with her, not with the workers making their way up the ramp with the supplies. "Understood." He motioned to Kenji and Shash, who followed him silently down the ramp onto the dock. They continued under *Phoenix's* wing to where *Vengeance* stood in the accompanying berth.

Seen side by side, the two ships were a study in contrasts. With its gold and red exterior and gliding winged configuration, *Phoenix* gave more than a nod to the mythical bird Natasha had named the ship after. By comparison, *Vengeance's* thick gunmetal grey plating and stocky outline resembled a rhinoceros. It could hit like one, too. Ships that faced off against *Vengeance* didn't fare well.

Each "leg" of the ship contained a cargo area, while *Vengeance's* "belly" formed the transport bay, allowing the ship's smaller attack vessels to enter and exit while concealed and protected by the four legs and the massive bay doors.

Isin strode into the shadows underneath the ship, the familiar hulk surrounding him like the walls of a cave. A rectangular patch of light from one of the portside cargo bays appeared as a ramp descended. A muscular man who'd been standing sentinel to the side of the entrance moved to intercept them.

"Sweep." Isin nodded at his head of security, the light from the cargo bay picking out the sprinkling of grey in his short dark hair and the lines grooved on his face from two decades of mercenary work.

"Welcome back."

"Good to be here." He turned to Shash. "Get started on the diagnostics."

She nodded, intense focus replacing the sour expression she'd had on *Phoenix.*

"Kenji, stow your gear then head for the commercial sector. If you run into any problems, alert Natasha before taking action."

"Aye, Cap." Kenji trotted after Shash.

Sweep gestured to *Phoenix*'s berth. "That's quite a ship you acquired. From the stories you've been telling me, I'd expected more of a derelict, and a little less—"

"Paint?"

The ghost of a smile crossed Sweep's face. "I gather the red and gold weren't your idea."

"No. The gold was already there. Natasha added the red." Which he didn't object to on principle, but when a mercenary ship used red, it was designed to look like blood, not plumage on an exotic bird.

"I see." Now Sweep sounded like he was swallowing a laugh. He moved to the control panel to retract the ramp and seal the door. When it closed with a soft thump, he turned back to Isin. "What can you tell me about our situation? The reception we received from port control was... interesting."

Isin ran his hand over his head. "Natasha has a history here. The authorities believe she's a captive of one of the Setarip factions, working under their orders, and that we're the newest recruits. As long as they keep believing that, we'll be leaving here with free supplies."

"How do we maintain that fiction?"

"With this." He showed Sweep the collar. "The Setarips control me, I control the crew. Natasha's convinced that's all it will take, but to be safe, I want you to be the only one who has any communication with the dock workers. And no one leaves the ship except Kenji, Itorye, and myself."

"Understood." Sweep's gaze grew speculative. "You're putting a lot of faith in Natasha. Do you trust her that much?"

His hands closed into fists. "She saved my *life*."

Sweep didn't flinch at the sharp look Isin gave him. "Not what I asked."

And he had no clear answer. Trust and Natasha were a complicated mix. She'd put her life on the line to save his, which had led to her year of captivity with the Setarips. He owed her a debt he wasn't sure he could ever repay. Unfortunately, the one thing she wanted was the *Phoenix*. She'd even been prepared to steal if out from under him while they were on Troi.

But he'd promised the ship to his crew. Giving it to Natasha could lead to a violent mutiny and both their deaths. He should know. It's how he'd gotten control of *Vengeance* in the first place.

He was only certain of one thing. "She'd only turn on me if I put her in a no-win scenario."

"You're sure about that?" Sweep and Itorye knew the full story about his history with Natasha, but neither of them had ever met her.

"Yes." And if he was wrong, he'd deal with the consequences.

Sweep held his gaze for several long moments. "Good to know."

Four

Isin ducked into his cabin to stow his belongings on his way to the bridge. A light on the comm panel flashed, indicating a waiting message. He checked the display. It was a vidcom from his sister, Danai.

He hadn't communicated with her since he'd left for Troi. Not that the long silence was unusual. Ever since he'd signed on as a mercenary, he'd had trouble talking to his baby sister. He couldn't very well share the details of his job, and his work had become his whole life.

He dumped his bag on his bunk and eyed the comm with the wariness of a mongoose facing off with a cobra. Ridiculous. It was just a vidcom message. He didn't even have to respond to it right away. But tension coiled in his gut.

The brother Danai remembered as an ambitious young man with lofty goals and a clear path to reach them was gone. The demons that drove him now were a far cry from the naïve optimism that had characterized his youth. He didn't want to drag her into the darkness that surrounded him, but cutting her out of his life wasn't an option, either.

At least the money he made ensured she could live her dreams. That would never change.

His hand drifted to his holster, his fingers resting on the irregular-shaped piece of shrapnel sewn into the lining. Thanks to Natasha, he was still alive to watch out for his sister. Without her sacrifice, the shard would have cost him his life.

The medic on *Sphinx* had removed it from his calf after Mirko had pulled him out of the dunes on Troi. He'd kept it to honor his connection to Natasha, a continual reminder of his failure and her loss.

He'd never forget the fierce concentration on her face as she'd tended to his wounds. Or the fire and sass she'd shot at him when he'd been an ungrateful prick. He was damned lucky she hadn't killed him herself.

He'd been drawn to her from his first day aboard the *Sphinx*. She had a quick mind, the only person he hadn't been able to outwit. She'd lacked the formal education his former wealth had afforded him, but had still managed to become the most skilled pilot he'd ever met, and a fair engineer to boot. Given the opportunity, she might have become a Fleet pilot or engineer, or a scientist like Danai.

A faint smile curved his lips. Well, maybe not. Natasha had a rebellious streak that bucked authority. She wouldn't have tolerated the regimentation of the Fleet Academy or a university, whereas Danai thrived on it. But Natasha might have made it through flight school. She could be piloting for a commercial outfit with a hefty salary and paid time off rather than scrambling for a living skating on the wrong side of the law.

His gaze swept around the room, his smile turning into a mocking grimace. Then again, he was living proof a good education was no guarantee of financial stability.

His father's gambling addiction and his parents' untimely deaths had saddled Isin with the burden of repaying enormous debts he'd never known existed. He'd sold everything of value the family had owned and had worked for four years as an unpaid employee for the head of the criminal organization his father owed money to in order to settle the accounts and keep his sister in school. As long as he'd done his job well, his sister's tuition had been subsidized.

Danai had been unaware of the arrangement, which had been his intention. She'd believed her expenses were being paid by a trust set up by their parents that had been untouchable after their deaths. At sixteen, seeing the family's history sold off piece by piece had been hard enough on her, especially so soon after putting their parents to rest. He hadn't wanted her to know their father had gambled away their futures, too.

But two years ago she'd been offered a part-time position as a research assistant that had also included a stipend to cover half the cost of her tuition. He'd finally had a way out of his monetary prison. He'd left the organization and signed on with Mirko on the *Sphinx*. The job provided free room and board, allowing him to send all the money he earned to pay for the remainder of his sister's tuition and living expenses.

It had also come with an unexpected perk. Natasha. She'd been a ray of light in his dreary existence. Her sharp wit and unfailing can-do attitude had warmed him like sunshine whenever she walked into the room. He'd focused his brainpower on coming up with excuses to talk to her, even if it meant questioning her actions just so she'd argue with him. Since he'd been hired on as the ship's contract negotiator, Mirko had paired him with Natasha for cargo deliveries on a regular basis. He'd been delighted to sit in *Gypsy*'s co-pilot's seat. Natasha hadn't been nearly as pleased.

And with good reason. He'd been a waste of space, which he'd proven the day they'd encountered the Setarips at Troi. He still had nightmares, still heard the pounding of Natasha's feet on the stairs as she'd led the Setarips away from the torpedo tube where she'd insisted he hide. He'd forced his way out as soon as he'd realized what she was doing, but it had been too late. By the time he'd dragged his worthless carcass into the corridor, the ship had fallen deathly silent.

He'd stumbled and crawled down the passageway and up the staircase, determined to find out what had happened to her. He'd made it to one of the upper landings before his strength had failed him, an exhausted delirium taking over. He'd contacted Mirko for help, probably babbling like a lunatic. He had no memory of what he'd said, but it must have been enough to convince her to come find him. He'd passed out on the landing and woken up in the *Sphinx*'s infirmary. When he'd asked Mirko about Natasha, she'd told him with an irritated sniff that there'd been no sign of her or *Gypsy*.

He'd believed Natasha had died that day, and a part of his soul had died with her. What a shock to come face-to-face with her in the sandy dunes once again.

But that was Natasha. Indomitable.

Except she hadn't been. Not really. The Setarips had turned her into their puppet, the one the authorities of Gallows Edge feared. The cold lifelessness in her eyes and the lack of animation in her features since they'd arrived haunted him. He had to get her away from this worthless rock. Once he was calling the shots, he could protect her. But he had to win the bet first.

He glanced at the flashing light. Danai's message would have to wait.

Five

When Isin stepped onto the bridge, he found Itorye all alone, seated in the captain's chair at the center of the room. She rose with the fluidity of a dancer, a small smile on her lips as she descended the stairs of the captain's platform to meet him.

She was the tallest woman on the crew, standing almost at eye level with him when she wore the heeled boots she favored, as she did now. Most people noticed the beauty of her almond-shaped eyes and pale porcelain skin, rather than the powerhouse that dwelt within the graceful exterior. The man her parents had pledged her to had foolishly considered her a trophy to be paraded out for guests. She'd shown her parents and her fiancé the error of their ways, turning her back on her inheritance and her betrothal to pursue a future of her own making.

Their loss was Isin's gain. He couldn't ask for a better first mate.

He gestured to the elaborate loops and coils of dark hair piled on top of her head. "You changed the style." Last time he'd seen her, she'd been keeping her hair in braids.

"A new style for a new venture." She pointed to the panoramic bridgescreen, where a projected image of *Phoenix* filled one section. Unlike most vessels, the bridge for *Vengeance* was located in the center of the ship, rather than the front or top. Visibility was achieved not through viewports or a front-facing bridgescreen, but via a series of exterior cameras that projected a three-hundred-sixty-degree image surrounding the bridge.

Dock workers continued to flow in and out of *Phoenix*'s cargo hold. Natasha stood at her post on the ramp, her back straight and her gaze locked on the dock workers, who darted around her like frightened mice.

Isin was used to generating that kind of fear, but in his experience, Natasha had always preferred blending into the shadows. Stealth had been her strength, not intimidation. Seeing the freight crews reacting to her that way was unsettling.

Itorye gestured to the image. "Sweep just checked in. They've started loading our supplies."

"Good." He'd contacted her shortly after Natasha had spoken to the tower, giving her a brief explanation so she could prepare the crew for arrival.

She glanced at his neck. "Is that the collar you mentioned?"

"Yeah." He ran his fingers along the ridge. It was annoying him already, and it wasn't even real. Natasha had worn one that was lethal. Just thinking about it made his temperature rise. If Tnaryt wasn't already dead, he would—

"Isin?"

"What?"

She stared pointedly at his hand.

He was clutching the collar in his fist, his fingers digging into his palm. He released his grip.

"So we're supposed to be servants of the Setarips, correct?"

"That's right."

"Then how exactly do I explain why I'm inquiring about mercenary work?"

He and Natasha had discussed that while she'd been docking the ship. "Simple. The Setarips are expanding their influence. Just as the outpost is free to go about its business as long as they meet Tnaryt's demands, we're free to do mercenary work as long as we make the ships and crew available whenever he wants them."

"And they'll believe that?"

"These people fear the Setarips like the plague. They won't question anything that's remotely plausible."

"Then I'm glad you're the one who has to wear the collar. It wouldn't go with my outfit."

His lips turned up. "And that would be a crime." Itorye may have given up her privileged status, but she still dressed with class and sophistication. "Where are you headed?"

"The Cosmos Club."

"Sounds swanky."

"It is. I've been there before."

"Better you than me." His scar marked him as unfit for the aristocratic social set. "I'll be going with Natasha to a bar on the lower levels, and I sent Kenji to scout out weapons upgrades for *Phoenix*. What's the status of the crew?" He hadn't encountered anyone in the passageways except Avril, who'd been standing guard on D deck.

"Fleur and Avril are on security detail with Sweep, and Shash has Willow, Ranger, Pine, and Camp with her in the engine room. Byrd and Jake are on standby, and everyone else is in cabin lockdown."

"Any complaints?" He and Itorye didn't use cabin lockdown as a punishment as the previous captain had, but it was still an unpopular order.

"Not after I promised to open a keg in the rec hall as soon as we've secured our next assignment."

Leave it to Itorye to provide the perfect peace offering.

He glanced at the bridgescreen images. The exterior cameras provided a view of the workers loading the last few crates into *Vengeance*'s cargo hold, with Sweep supervising. Natasha was no longer visible, *Phoenix*'s bay now sealed, but he had no doubt she was monitoring the situation, probably from the pilot's chair on the bridge.

His comm device pinged a moment later. He opened the channel. "Isin."

"The loading's almost complete," Natasha said without preamble. "Pete and I will be heading out in a few minutes."

"We'll meet you on the dock." He closed the channel and gestured to Itorye, who followed him to the stairway.

"She's very clever, isn't she?"

"More than she knows." Her aptitude for flying and mechanical skills, picked up by observing others and hands-on practice, was unusual, something she didn't seem to realize. "She's a far better pilot than Byrd, even without formal training."

"Do you still want her working for you?"

More than anything. "Yes."

"We'll need to outwit her to win your bet."

He grunted.

"This will be a fascinating few days."

Fascinating wasn't the word he would use.

They exited into the cargo bay, where Sweep was looking over the stacks of supply crates. "Any issues?" Isin asked.

"Not a bit. But they almost tripped over their own feet getting out of here."

"That's a good sign." Intimidation was their ally in this game. "Alert me if anything changes."

"Aye."

Itorye walked with him down the ramp to the dock. Natasha stood beside *Vengeance* with Stevens, her gaze on Itorye as they approached, a frown line between her brows.

Itorye halted in front of her, not seeming the least bit put off by the cold look in Natasha's eyes. "It's a pleasure to finally meet you Captain Orlov."

Natasha hesitated a moment before responding. "I've heard a lot about you." Her gaze scanned Itorye from head to toe. "Is Itorye your first name or last name?"

"It's my only name."

"Only?"

"Yes. After my family disowned me, I stopped using their name." Itorye said it without rancor, but Natasha's eyes widened.

"I see." She glanced at Isin, questions lurking in her pale eyes. But she didn't ask them. "This is Pete Stevens, my engineer."

Stevens dipped his head slightly, almost shyly. "Pleasure to meet you, ma'am."

"You as well, Mr. Stevens."

"Oh, call me Pete. Most folks do."

"Very well, Pete."

A flash of annoyance crossed Natasha's face. "We should get going." She nodded to a sleek four-passenger vehicle parked beside *Phoenix*'s starboard wing.

Apparently supplies weren't the only item she could procure on Gallows Edge.

They headed toward the vehicle, but Isin halted several steps away, his hand dropping to the weapon at his hip. "Natasha, wait."

She tensed at the warning in his voice, palming her pistol. She followed the direction of his gaze as she backed slowly toward him. "Who is he?" She indicated the man leading the group of men and women walking toward them.

Itorye answered before Isin could. "Kerr." The name fell from her lips like a dead thing. She'd moved to Isin's other side, while Stevens flanked Natasha.

"Not a friend, I take it," Natasha murmured.

Isin shifted slightly so he was partially shielding Natasha with his body, but his gaze remained locked on *Vengeance*'s former first mate. "No."

Kerr sauntered toward them with the arrogance of a king approaching peasants.

Isin's finger itched. He had every reason to shoot Kerr on sight, but starting a firefight in the middle of the busy dock wasn't smart. Or prudent.

Kerr halted three meters away, his posse filling in behind him. His gaze traveled leisurely over Stevens, Natasha, and Itorye, before locking on Isin. "I see they allow vermin on this rock."

"Clearly." Isin stared him down. "You're here."

Kerr's lip lifted in a sneer. "Watch your mouth, traitor."

"Traitor?" Isin laughed without humor. "I provided a public service."

"You killed our captain."

"Shim wasn't a captain. He was a parasite. Like you." And Isin had allowed them to feed off him for nine months. If it hadn't been for Sweep and Itorye, they'd *still* be feeding off him.

Kerr's gaze flicked to Itorye. "Still the captain's whore, I see."

Isin's fingers twitched, but Itorye smiled. "Sour grapes, Kerr?"

A flush spread over his face. "Don't flatter yourself." His gaze moved to Natasha and Stevens. "And you've picked up some space trash. Did you pull these two out of the sewer?"

Stevens took a step forward, but Isin lifted an arm to stop him. Kerr wanted a reaction. The only way to handle him was not to give him one.

Stevens shot a look at Isin, but he moved back next to Natasha.

"Oh, so well trained. I commend you, Isin. Tell me, is the little chit your maid?" He lifted his chin to indicate Natasha. "Or is she here to service you?"

Flames ripped through Isin's veins. His finger closed on the trigger for his weapon.

"Isin." Itorye placed a restraining hand on his arm.

A clipped male voice cut through the tension. "Is there a problem here?"

Isin glanced to his right. A burly man with a flattened nose and a piercing through his eyebrow strode toward them, his hand resting on the holstered weapon of his dock security uniform. A squad of additional personnel fanned out behind him, their weapons drawn and aimed at Kerr's group.

The man halted, facing Kerr. "I said, is there a problem here?"

Kerr's gaze shifted to the security officer, the malevolence in his eyes replaced with idle curiosity and a benign smile. "No problem. We're just catching up."

"Catching up?" The officer's tone conveyed what he thought of that reply. "This conversation is over."

Kerr lifted his hands. "I don't want any trouble, officer." His expression conveyed sincerity, but the officer clearly wasn't buying it.

"Move along."

"Of course." Kerr nodded, his gaze meeting Isin's as he turned. "Until next time." Motioning to his followers, he strode down the dock, parting the flow of traffic like a shark cutting through a school of fish.

Several of the security personnel followed at a discreet distance.

The officer turned to Natasha. "I apologize for the inconvenience."

She nodded, her expression the same arctic mask she'd used with the port authorities and dock workers.

"I'll post personnel here to—"

"That won't be necessary." Her gaze shifted briefly to Isin. "We can handle it."

They needed to handle it. They couldn't afford to have the security personnel watching closely enough to figure out Natasha wasn't with the Setarips anymore.

The officer seemed displeased by her response, but he didn't argue. "As you wish. Please let me know if you encounter any more trouble." The remaining security staff followed him as he retreated in the direction of the tram station.

The security officer must have been watching Natasha from the moment she'd stepped onto the dock. "Are they always this quick to intervene?"

She met his gaze. "They are with me."

His comm device chimed. Pulling it out of his pocket, he opened the channel.

Sweep's voice came over the line. "I see Kerr paid a visit."

Isin glanced at *Vengeance.* Sweep stood in the opening between the forward and aft cargo bays, a rifle slung over his shoulder. Avril and Fleur waited a few steps behind, rifles at the ready.

"Dock security is watching him. We shouldn't have any more trouble." One more complication they didn't need. "But keep an eye on the docks and *Phoenix.*"

"Understood."

Kerr on Gallows Edge. What were the odds? Isin turned to Natasha and gestured to the transport. "Shall we?"

Six

Itorye and Stevens settled into the backseat while Isin crammed himself in beside Natasha. The vehicle was a sporty model more fitting for open road driving rather than the limited confines of Gallows Edge. It didn't provide much headroom either, which forced him to pull his knees up to his chest and scrunch down in his seat. Even so, the textured material of the ceiling brushed the bare skin on top of his head. He struggled to fasten the safety harness. "They didn't have anything larger?"

Natasha started the vehicle. "They know I like fast cars." A hint of amusement shone in her pale eyes. "I assume you wouldn't prefer to ride in the back of a cargo truck?"

"No." But Natasha seemed to be enjoying seeing him stuffed in like a baby in the womb. He glanced back at Itorye, who managed to look completely comfortable and composed in the small space.

Natasha's hands gripped the steering wheel as she threw the vehicle into motion, shoving him back in his seat.

Fast car was right. She was racing down the concourse like her tail was on fire. Other vehicles moved to the side ahead of them, clearing a path.

"How do they know—"

"Alert signal. A warning displays on their consoles whenever my vehicle's in motion. They get out of the way if they don't want to deal with outpost security."

"You get full service here."

"For now. But the longer we're here, the greater the risk."

"And if they find out the Setarips are gone?"

"We'll be lucky to make it off this rock alive."

She slowed as they approached the central hub. Passengers were queued in front of the main lifts, but Natasha swerved to the right, zipping down a winding ramp that led to the next level. She brought the car to a halt next to the wide boulevard leading into a utilitarian commercial district. A similar but slightly more affluent boulevard opened on the opposite side of the lifts across a bridge. She glanced at Stevens. "You'll find the parts retailers down there." She pointed to the right. "Let me know if you learn anything promising."

Stevens grinned as he opened his door. "Oh, I will."

Itorye had opened her door as well. She met Isin's gaze before stepping out. "I'll be in touch."

He nodded, watching as she strode down the walkway toward the bridge, drawing appreciative glances from passersby.

A subtle tapping sound drew his attention.

Natasha's gaze was locked on Itorye, her thumb drumming on the steering wheel with the irritated rhythm of a cat twitching its tail. When she realized he was watching her, she immediately stopped and put the vehicle into gear, gunning down the street toward a row of larger cargo lifts. She touched a button on the dashboard. "Open cargo number four."

A red light flashed over the top of one of the cargo lifts and the doors slid open.

She halted the vehicle inside the lift. "Level twelve."

The doors closed and the lift started to descend.

She faced him, her eyes shooting darts. "You want to tell me what that was all about?"

"What?"

"That scene on the dock."

He'd already pushed the incident to the back of his mind, focusing on the task at hand. Apparently she hadn't. He shrugged as much as his cramped position allowed. "Not right now."

Natasha's eyes grew glacial. "Halt lift."

The lift gave a little jolt as its downward motion ceased.

He frowned. "Natasha, we don't have time—"

"Wrong." She focused on him like a laser. "Let me rephrase. Tell me what that was all about or we won't be leaving this lift." The stubborn set of her jaw indicated she meant business.

Rehashing how he'd become captain of *Vengeance* wasn't on his agenda. Now that he knew Kerr was in residence, he was even more determined to win the wager and get off this rock as soon as possible. But he'd have to give Natasha some background if he wanted her cooperation.

She settled into her seat and folded her arms, her gaze never leaving his.

He sighed. "Kerr is *Vengeance's* former first mate."

"But not yours."

"No." The very idea made his blood boil. "He was in that position when I signed on."

"He said you killed the previous captain. Is that true?" Natasha's eyes were intent, but she didn't seem horrified by the possibility.

"It's true."

"What happened?"

Isin stared at the closed doors of the lift. How much should he share? "When I signed onto *Vengeance,* I was hostile, bitter, full of rage. I didn't care who I worked for, what I did. I welcomed a brutal environment where I could work out my... frustrations." He paused, drawing a breath as echoes of the past shoved their way into the present.

"Go on." Her voice was calm, encouraging. She seemed to be taking it in stride.

"I did what I was told. Fought anyone who crossed my path. Lost more often than I won. Earned this." He drew his forefinger along the scar that marked his right cheek. He'd told Jake to use sutures to seal it so that it would have a raised, aggressive appearance after it healed. Jake had protested, wanting to minimize any permanent damage, but he'd relented when Isin had refused to let him treat him otherwise. "I enjoyed the abuse I received, and the pain I caused others. At least, at first."

"What changed?"

"I met Sweep."

"He's in charge of security on *Vengeance*, right?"

"He is now. But when I first signed on, Shim, the man I killed, had left him to rot in the ship's brig."

"Why?"

"He'd fought against Shim and Kerr when they spaced the previous captain and seized control of *Vengeance*."

Natasha's lips parted in surprise. "Your ship changes hands frequently."

"It's not uncommon with mercenary crews."

"Hmm." The look in her eyes spoke volumes. "How did you and Sweep meet?"

"One of my duties as a grunt was taking rations to the prisoners. What Shim gave Sweep was barely enough to keep him alive. He was emaciated, painful to even look at, although I didn't care at first." No, he'd let the situation continue, complicit in his silence. But the torment hadn't dimmed the fierceness of Sweep's gaze, or the dignity with which he'd held himself when Isin had delivered his meager food.

"During one of Shim's mercurial fits, he punished me for a trumped up offense and threw me into Sweep's cell. I reacted like a caged tiger, banging on the bars and growling at Sweep. I think Shim wanted to see if I'd kill him."

"But you didn't."

"No. If Sweep had reacted, shown fear, I might have." He'd been in a dark place, almost out of his mind with hate. "But he just watched me, calm as a Buddha." A thin, weak Buddha.

And that serenity had knocked him out of the path he'd been barreling along. "We ended up staring at each other for days, not saying a word, until Shim decided to let me out. The next time I delivered food to the cells, I added part of my daily ration to what I gave Sweep." Sweep had gazed at the food, and at him, with that same serenity, almost as if he'd expected it. He'd given a small nod of gratitude before eating.

"And you became friends?"

"Yes." After their faceoff in the brig, day by day Sweep had drawn the story of Natasha out of him like he was pulling venom from a wound. When he'd told him everything there was to say, every painful, soul-crushing detail, Sweep had given him a look full of compassion and understanding, and said the words that had struck him worse than any blow, galvanizing him into action. *If you allow your guilt to destroy you, then her sacrifice meant nothing.*

"Shim and Kerr didn't visit the cells, so they never suspected. For months I shared my food, until the day I was able to free him and stage a coup. By then, he looked a lot less like a walking skeleton."

"The two of you took over the ship by yourselves?"

"No." Although it was gratifying that she believed he was capable of that feat. "I also had Itorye on my side."

Natasha's jaw flexed. "What was your relationship with her?"

It took a moment to catch her meaning. "Not what you're thinking. She'd been friends with Sweep back before Shim and Kerr took over *Vengeance.* When she figured out I was helping him, she started trusting me, making me aware of what we were facing."

"Which was?"

"Experts at manipulation. She'd been the first mate until Shim and Kerr had betrayed the captain. They'd convinced the majority of the crew that he was skimming money from their earnings. Once the crew believed, Kerr and Shim took over the ship, installing themselves as captain and first mate. Anyone who opposed them was spaced or imprisoned."

"What about Itorye? How did she survive?"

"They were smart enough to know she'd be a threat when the fighting started, so they locked her in her cabin while she was sleeping. Shim had a thing for her, so after it was over, he offered her the option to stay on... with him."

Natasha's fingers gripped her biceps. "And she agreed?"

He didn't detect condemnation in her tone. More like understanding. "She's a survivor. She knew she could outwit him eventually. By the time she decided I was the one who could help her get the job done, several members of the crew were as eager as we were to get out from under Shim's thumb."

A line creased the space between Natasha's brows. "Why didn't Itorye take over as captain?"

"She didn't want to."

"Why not?"

"She's happier as first mate. She made it clear she wanted me to be captain."

Natasha gave a little harrumph and shifted to face forward. Her jaw looked carved from granite. "How perfect for you."

Isin studied her. She looked annoyed. No, she looked *angry.* "Do you have a problem with Itorye?"

"Why would I have a problem with her?"

"You tell me. Your eyes are shooting daggers."

She blinked, her chest rising and falling as she took a deep breath. And changed the subject. "So you killed Shim, but Kerr got away?"

She was evading. He'd let her, for now. "Unfortunately. Kerr and one of our pilots stole a transport while I was fighting Shim. Sweep tried to shoot them down, but Kerr had disabled *Vengeance's* weapons."

"And now he's here." Natasha rested her hands on the steering wheel. "How dangerous is he?"

"Lethal. He prefers to stab you in the back rather than face a fair fight, and he uses persuasion and manipulation to win people over to his side. He can be charming when it serves his purposes. Those he's drawn in tend to follow his orders blindly."

"Did you recognize the people with him?"

"Only the pilot. But he's clearly made some new friends."

"He'd be a fool to try anything overt while we're here. But if he's fond of sneak attacks—"

"He could still pose a threat. I know." It was an unwelcome complication. "Sweep understands him better than anyone. We'll handle it."

She shot him a quick look before reengaging the lift. "I have no doubt."

Seven

The lift came to a stop and the doors opened. Natasha took off again, but at a more sedate pace than on the boulevard. The roadway was a lot narrower, more of an alley than a road, actually, that was probably only used for delivery and refuse collection. The original mining tunnels had been converted, the curved wall to the left giving the alley an asymmetrical shape.

They passed the back doors for a row of businesses on their right, the block walls grungy compared to what he'd seen on the upper levels. Then again, he was seeing a part of the outpost most visitors didn't. The main entrances might be better maintained.

Natasha swung the vehicle in a tight turn behind one of the non-descript edifices, bringing it to face the lift at the far end of the alley.

Isin unfastened his harness as she cut the motor, but paused with his hand on the door handle when he realized Natasha hadn't moved. Her gaze was locked on the door to their left, where DOOHAN'S was stenciled in simple block letters.

"Natasha?"

She gave a little jerk, like she'd forgotten he was in the car with her. "What?"

"Is something wrong?"

"Wrong?" The arctic façade she'd had on the docks settled over her features like mist. "No. Let's go." She was out of the vehicle in a flash, striding toward the marked door, her dark brown duster swirling around her like a cape. He extricated himself from the cramped confines, catching up as she pulled open the back door like she was charging into battle.

He followed as she disappeared into the dimly lit hallway. The clicks and clatters from gaming tables and the murmur of conversation drifted toward him from the archway at the end.

Stepping through the archway, he scanned his surroundings. The room opened up in front of him, filled with an assortment of tables, a long bar to the left, and gaming tables at the far end. Natasha headed straight for the bar, settling onto one of the empty stools at the near end.

Several of the customers glanced at her, their expressions a mixture of wariness, fear, and disgust. Those seated nearby moved to the opposite end of the bar, leaving all the stools in her vicinity vacant. Apparently her connection to the Setarips was well known to the general populace, not just the outpost authorities.

But one person had the opposite reaction. The bartender stopped mid-pour, abandoning the beer mug in his hand. He grabbed a clean glass from a rack under the counter, filled it with amber liquid, and hurried down to where Natasha sat.

Isin slid onto the stool to her right as the bartender set the mug down on the counter.

"Lass! It's good ta' see ya' here." The bartender's gaze shifted to Isin, giving him a quick once over.

Natasha gestured between them. "Isin, Doohan. Doohan, Isin."

Doohan's eyes widened slightly at her casual introduction. He gave a brief nod at Isin before returning his attention to Natasha. "I'll be right back." He quickly returned to where he'd left the half-filled beer glass, topped it off, and handed it to the waiting customer before rejoining Natasha. "I was beginning ta' worry."

"I'm fine. Better than fine, actually." She dropped her voice to a murmur. "I'm free."

Doohan's chubby face creased in a wide smile. "Are you now?"

She nodded.

He lowered his voice so Isin could barely make out his words over the background noise of the bar. "It was the woman, wasn't it? The one askin' about the Setarips?"

"Yes. She saved my life."

The bartender beamed. "I had a good feelin' about her."

"You were right."

His gaze shifted to her neck, and he frowned. "But you're still wearin—"

"It's a fake. I couldn't come back without it."

"Ah." Doohan nodded in understanding, his attention moving to Isin. "And how do you know the lass?"

"We're old friends."

Natasha snorted.

Doohan glanced at her, his expression losing some of its cheerfulness. "That so?"

Isin fixed him with a piercing stare. "Yes."

Most men quailed under such scrutiny, but Doohan held his ground. Then again, he ran a bar in the lower levels of Gallows Edge. He was probably used to receiving threats. And he seemed very fond of Natasha.

She eyed them both. "You can knock off the testosterone competition." She focused on Doohan. "Isin and I have an arrangement."

"Do ya' now?" Doohan's look darkened. "What kinda arrangement?"

"Nothing like that. A profitable one. I'm looking to pick up a large cargo haul."

Doohan's brows lifted. "Cargo haul?" He rested his forearms on the counter. "And ya' need ta' keep the port authority in the dark, I suppose."

"Definitely."

Doohan rubbed his chin. "How large a cargo can *Gypsy* handle?"

"Actually, I'm flying a converted passenger freighter, and Isin's warship is even larger. Together we could haul just about anything."

Doohan's brows climbed nearly to his receding hairline. "And the authorities didna question ya' when you arrived with two new ships?"

Natasha smirked. "I indicated the ships were allied with the Setarips. They didn't question that."

"No, I suspect they wouldna." Doohan pushed back from the counter. "Well, you're in the right spot. I get asked regular about reliable freighters."

Isin bit back a groan. His suspicions were correct. Natasha had worked this situation to her advantage. He couldn't let that go unchallenged. "Do you get anyone in here looking to hire mercenaries?"

Natasha glared at him, but he ignored her.

Doohan's gaze darted to the scar on Isin's cheek. "Would that be your specialty?"

Isin inclined his head. "Know anyone looking to hire a crew?"

Doohan glanced at Natasha, who had her head down as she stared into her mug. His expression shuttered. "Nothin' comes to mind."

Isin's eyes narrowed. He was lying. But he couldn't fault him for it. Clearly Doohan was loyal to Natasha, and her body language made it clear she wasn't happy with Isin's line of questioning.

Isin placed a credit square on the counter. "Then why don't you bring me a mug of what she's having? I'll cover hers, too." If he wasn't going to make progress talking to Doohan, he'd need a drink in his hand while he worked the room.

Natasha hunched her shoulders. "I'll pay for my own damn drink."

Doohan's chest expanded like a bellows. "You'll pay for nothin' at all." He nodded at the mug in her hand. "It's on the house."

"But Doohan—"

"No buts, lass. You deserve far more than a drink after what you've been through."

Isin was inclined to agree. And much as Natasha's manipulation of the situation irked him, he appreciated Doohan's kindness to her. Natasha hadn't been completely isolated from a friendly face during her time with the Setarips.

Doohan's gaze shifted to Isin and he plucked the credit square off the counter. "I'll get your drink."

His generosity clearly did not extend to Isin.

As soon as the bartender moved away, Isin faced Natasha. "Loading the deck?"

She stared after Doohan. "What do you mean?"

"You picked this outpost because it gives you an advantage."

She shrugged. "Only if there's someone looking to run freight. And assuming I can arrange it without alerting the authorities." She met his gaze. "I'm trusting you not to tell them."

The comment hit him in the solar plexus. It hadn't even occurred to him that she was taking a huge chance bringing him here. If he acted like a typical mercenary, he could make a lot of money and gain control of both ships simply by alerting the authorities to her changed situation. The provisions they had loaded onto *Phoenix* and *Vengeance* must have cost the outpost residents a pretty penny. He could claim a reward for freeing them from that obligation.

But the very idea brought bile into his throat. He swallowed it back down. "I would never betray you."

Her gaze searched his for a long moment. "I hope not." She sighed, the wariness in her eyes fading away, leaving an emptiness that was much worse. "I didn't realize how much being back here would affect me."

"Do you want to leave?"

She shook her head. "It's the best place to find work. For either of us."

"Then we'll stay."

He needed to check in with Itorye, see if she was having any luck at the Cosmos Club.

Doohan returned with his drink, setting it on the bar with a solid thunk and placing the credit square beside it. A quick glance indicated a significant deduction on the square's balance. Either Doohan had overcharged him on purpose, or he'd decided to let Isin pay for Natasha's drink after all.

Isin lifted the mug and took a sip. The brew had an earthy quality and a slightly bitter aftertaste, but it wasn't bad. He brought the mug with him as he slid off the stool. "I'll check back with you in a bit," he murmured to Natasha.

She waved him off, continuing her conversation with Doohan.

Ducking into an alcove near the kitchen, he set his drink on a low wall and pulled his comm device from his pocket.

Itorye responded after a few seconds. "Problem?"

"Just checking in. Any news?"

"Not so far. Everyone I've spoken with either has their own private security forces in place, or they're not currently planning anything that would require our services."

"Keep trying."

"Does the concern in your voice indicate Orlov's making progress obtaining a cargo haul?"

"She has a local connection who's helping her locate one."

"Oh, really?" Itorye sounded vaguely amused. "Clever woman. I'll let you know if I get any leads."

"Do that." A lot was riding on this.

Eight

Itorye obviously didn't share his concern regarding how the crew would react if he lost this bet. They might be okay making the cargo run—it would still pay well—but taking orders from Natasha? His crew followed him because they feared and respected him. If they learned he'd been outmaneuvered by his petite companion, they could decide he wasn't worthy of either.

He spent the next half hour circulating through the room, gauging the bar's clientele. The regulars were easy to pick out. They had a settled quality to their behavior that the visitors did not. A woman with dyed red hair and a serious case of overconfidence had approached him offering paid companionship. A pointed look had sent her moving on, but not before she'd given him a saucy smile and a murmured "You'll change your mind" as she strolled off.

He'd spent some time in the gaming room, making use of his negotiation skills to get the patrons to share information, but hadn't found anyone who could provide him with a lead on a mercenary job. Hopefully Natasha wasn't having any luck, either.

She'd chosen to remain at the bar, which surprised him. Sitting alone at the far end wasn't likely to bring her in contact with anyone. And yet, when he returned to get a refill on his drink, he found a woman seated to her left, their heads bent in conversation.

The woman was dressed in a dark brown jumpsuit, with a matching work cap pulled low over her forehead. As he drew closer, he spotted an orange sanitation logo embroidered on the front of the cap and the breast pocket of the jumpsuit. The woman gave him a furtive look and visibly tensed.

Natasha glanced over her shoulder and frowned, then turned back to the woman and make a dismissive gesture, the non-verbal equivalent of *don't worry about him.*

Isin's jaw clenched. He didn't appreciate being dismissed, verbally *or* non-verbally. He caught Doohan's attention and lifted his empty glass. The bartender gave a short nod, grabbing a mug and filling it.

Isin leaned his forearm on the counter behind Natasha.

She shot him a look of annoyance.

The woman's gaze shifted from Natasha to him, her eyes widening and her chest rising and falling with badly concealed agitation as she stared at his scar.

He was used to that reaction, but the look in her brown eyes spoke of more than fear. Intelligence shone through, as though she were analyzing him for his constituent parts. She seemed... bookish, which didn't jibe with the evidence that she worked as a manual laborer. Her light brown skin showed faint creases around her eyes, indicating she was in her late thirties to early forties.

A thump on the bar beside his elbow drew his attention. Doohan had plunked his drink down and was leaning toward him with his hands braced on the counter's edge. "Problem?" The question came out as a warning.

Isin favored him with a small smile. "Not at all."

Doohan gestured to the full mug. "There's your drink." The *now get lost* was implied.

Isin reached into his pocket and slid a credit square on the counter. "Add twenty percent for yourself."

Doohan's mouth turned down and he glanced at Natasha. At her brief nod, he swept up the credit square and retreated from the battle.

Natasha turned her head to meet Isin's gaze. The message in that look was loud and clear. *Don't mess this up.*

He inclined his head slightly before refocusing his attention on the woman. "I'm Elhadj Isin. Natasha's... associate."

The woman glanced between them. Again, he had the sensation of being visually dissected. "Abbey Green."

And I'm the head of the Galactic Fleet. He'd been in this situation enough times to have anticipated she'd give him an alias. He also picked up on a slight accent, one she was trying very hard to conceal. Paired with her coloring, he'd guess she had roots in southeastern Asia.

"She's looking to hire a couple ships." Natasha's mouth tilted up like the cat who'd eaten the canary. "For a cargo run."

Several earthy swear words swirled behind Isin's tongue, but he kept them contained by taking a drink from the mug Doohan had delivered. He hadn't lost this fight yet. "What's the destination?" If it was nearby, the job might not meet the agreed upon minimum.

Natasha glanced back at Green, whose gaze settled on Isin.

Her eyes narrowed. Ignoring the question, she posed one of her own. "What's your role in this operation?"

A negotiation. He could play this game with his eyes closed. "I'm captain of *Vengeance.* A mercenary warship."

"They provide muscle when needed." Natasha shot him another warning look. "I'm captain of *Phoenix.* The passenger freighter I mentioned."

Green glanced between them, assessing. "I see."

"We can split up the cargo between the two ships if necessary, depending on what you need transported."

Green pinned Isin with a hard stare. "How many on your crew?"

"Twenty-one."

"All mercenaries?"

"Except for my medic."

"And is your crew loyal? Trustworthy?"

Isin met her stare for stare. "As long as they get paid."

Green's lips pursed, her gaze shifting to Natasha. "And what about your crew?"

"Definitely trustworthy. We're not mercenaries. We're freight runners."

The silent condemnation in her tone loosened Isin's tongue. "And smugglers and thieves."

Natasha kicked his leg with the heel of her boot. "Only if the job requires it." She glared at him over her shoulder.

But Green's reaction wasn't what he'd expected. Rather than being dismayed by his comment, she was looking at Natasha with increased interest. "So you have experience avoiding unwanted... attention?"

Natasha blinked, looking as surprised as he was. "Yes."

"Very good." Green nodded. "I'll travel on your ship." Her gaze shifted to Isin. "Your crew will be in charge of obtaining the cargo."

"Obtaining?" Isin's eyes narrowed. "What do you mean, obtaining?" Maybe this was a mercenary job after all.

"You will need to fetch the cargo from its current location. We will travel ahead and meet you at the final destination."

"We won't be traveling together?" Cargo transports often flew in convoys to decrease the chance of problems from Setarips... or mercenaries. He didn't like the idea of losing sight of the *Phoenix*. Or Natasha.

"No. The ships must travel separately."

"And where is this cargo?"

"I will provide you with the details later."

"You'll provide us with the details now or it's no deal." He'd just seen his loophole out of this situation and he dove through it.

"I cannot."

"And I won't make an agreement without all the facts."

Natasha shifted on her stool. "He's right. We can't settle on a price for the job until we know the destination. *All* the destinations."

Green's expression reminded him of some of his more stoic university professors when a student argued against them. "I assure you, the rewards will be well worth your efforts." She named a price that made Isin's jaw hinge open.

Natasha seemed similarly stunned.

So much for his loophole. If his crew would be that well compensated, they likely wouldn't have any complaints about the assignment or having Natasha in charge of the operation. They'd be too busy figuring out how they were going to spend the flood of money dropping into their laps. It also confirmed that Green certainly wasn't a sanitation worker.

"I'll pay you half before we leave the outpost, and the other half when both ships arrive at our destination."

Natasha found her voice first. "How long will this take?"

"If your ships have any speed at all, you should be able to make the trip in two weeks."

Two weeks. It was an exorbitant price for such a short time commitment. "What's the catch?"

Green met his gaze. "Catch?"

"You could hire six ships for that price. Why so much? What aren't you telling us?"

She drew in a slow breath. "I am paying extra for your discretion. It is imperative that our movements go unnoticed. By anyone."

So she wasn't just hiding from the Fleet. She had personal enemies as well. Which brought up another important question. "Is the cargo hazardous?" A cascade of money wouldn't do his crew any good if they all died before they delivered it.

Green shook her head. "I assure you, the cargo does not pose a danger to your crew."

The muscles around Natasha's eyes tensed slightly. He knew that look. She was determining whether Green was lying. She glanced over her shoulder and raised her brows. Her expression indicated she believed the cargo itself was safe. Transporting it, however, might put them at risk.

That wasn't a problem for him. The job was sounding more like mercenary work all the time, something he intended to point out if they took it. They'd made a lot of strange deliveries together while working on the *Sphinx*. They could handle this.

He gave a subtle nod. Their client was hiding most of her cards, but he could play her game. One way or another, they'd come out on top.

"Our discretion is guaranteed," Natasha said, turning back to Green. "When do you want to leave?"

"As soon as possible."

"Four hours?"

"Fine."

So much for making upgrades to *Phoenix's* weapons system before they left.

"*Phoenix* is at docking berth A14."

"I will want to see *Vengeance* as well."

"Okay." Natasha sounded like she was tamping down irritation. "It's in the next berth, A15."

Green stood. "I'll see you at the dock." Pulling her cap down to shadow her eyes, she headed for the entrance at a brisk clip.

Natasha watched her go, her gaze speculative. "She's not a very good liar. And she knows it."

"What makes you say that?"

She took a sip from her mug. "Because she evaded questions rather than making something up."

"There are a lot of unknowns on this job."

"Yep."

"And it may require as much mercenary work as cargo work."

Natasha snorted. "You don't know that."

"No, but it seems likely."

She gave him a sidelong glance. "Meaning what?"

"Meaning we may have to call this particular wager a draw."

"A draw?"

He nodded. "Since we won't be traveling together, you'll be in charge of your crew, and I'll be in charge of mine." And the question of who owned *Phoenix* would be tabled for a while longer.

She studied him for a moment. "You don't want to tell your crew you lost."

"That's beside the point."

"That's exactly the point. So I'll agree that you should be in charge of your crew for the trip. That's logical. But I found the client. I won the bet. I'm still calling the shots."

And by the stubborn set of her jaw, she wasn't budging from that position. She knew she had him, and nothing he said would change her mind.

At least his crew wouldn't find out he'd lost. "Fine."

She slid off her stool. "Then let's go. We can talk about the details on the way."

Nine

While Natasha said goodbye to Doohan, Isin sent a quick message to Itorye informing her that they had a job. She replied that she'd meet him back at the ship in an hour.

Natasha drove at a more sedate pace on the way back to the lift. She tapped her thumbs on the steering wheel as they started their ascent. "I'm trying to decide if she's a corporate executive who embezzled secrets or assets, or a wealthy socialite who got herself on the wrong side of something she can't handle."

He grunted. "She's definitely in over her head. But as long as she comes through with the money, I don't care who she is."

"You don't?"

"No."

"Then you're not worried that the job will get... complicated?"

He fixed her with a baleful look. "Have we ever worked a job together that *didn't* get complicated?"

The hint of a smile finally broke through her grim expression. "No."

He shrugged. "Then why worry?" It was a waste of time and energy. His experiences on *Vengeance* had taught him that. But he'd plan every detail to the letter and inspect their cargo with a fine-toothed comb.

The muscles around her mouth twitched and her eyes sparkled, like she was fighting back a grin.

He frowned. "What?"

Her teeth flashed as she lost the battle. "I just never thought I'd see the day."

"What are you talking about?"

"You. A year ago you would have been pestering me the entire drive back with questions I couldn't answer about who she was and what she was up to. I never expected you to be so... accepting."

"A lot of things have changed in the past year."

She was silent for a moment. When she responded, her voice had lost all trace of mirth. "Yes, they have." The lift came to a stop and the doors parted. Natasha pulled out and joined the flow of vehicles on the main boulevard. She picked up speed, the cars beginning to move out of her path as they had before. "Do you have plenty of storage space on *Vengeance* for whatever she wants you to haul?"

"Yes." The ship's cargo holds contained their assault vehicles, extra munitions, and spare parts for ship and vehicle repairs, but that still left sufficient space for their client's unknown cargo. They could always transfer smaller items to the upper decks to create more room if necessary.

He was far more concerned about the defenses on *Phoenix.* "I'll have Kenji restock *Phoenix*'s armory before we take off. We won't have time to install the upgrades to the ship's weapons."

"I was thinking about that, too." Her mouth turned down. "I'd say we have a better than fifty percent chance someone's going to try to intercept our cargo or waylay our passenger before we reach our destination."

"Agreed." And unlike *Vengeance, Phoenix* wasn't designed for battle... yet. "That's why I'll be sending some of my crew over to *Phoenix.*"

She glanced at him, her eyes narrowing. "Oh?"

"You need security and weapons personnel. Stevens is going to be busy in the engine room, and you'll be flying the ship. That leaves Brooks, and we both know he's no fighter."

She grimaced. "No, he's not." She kept her gaze forward as they passed the rows of docked ships. "Who did you have in mind?"

"Kenji, for one." He was trustworthy and had already started to bond with the crew. He'd watch out for Natasha, too. "Fleur and Avril are both good in a fight. And honorable." Unlike most of his crew, who were motivated by monetary gain, Fleur and Avril wouldn't turn on Natasha if things got rough.

She pulled the vehicle to a halt in front of *Phoenix.* "I can live with that."

Good thing. He hadn't planned to give her a choice.

Ten

"She's here."

Isin glanced over his shoulder at Itorye. "Natasha?"

"Green."

He checked the bridge's chronometer. Still two hours until their agreed upon departure time. She was antsier than he'd realized. "Where is she?"

"In the cargo hold with Sweep."

Then she was in good hands. Sweep had the patience of a saint. He'd take care of whatever she wanted.

"She's demanding to speak to you."

Or not. He pushed out of the captain's chair and headed off the bridge. "Tell Sweep I'm on my way."

As soon as he reached the cargo bay, voices drifted toward him from the direction of the closed bay door. To his right, Shorty and Summer were securing the stacks of munitions crates Kenji had delivered. Summer tilted her head in the direction of the clipped female voice and rolled her eyes.

Isin was inclined to agree with her assessment. He was grateful that Green would be Natasha's responsibility, not his.

"And does the entire crew have access to the cargo bay?" Green's back was to Isin as he approached. She'd traded the maintenance uniform for a dark grey flight jumpsuit and matching skullcap.

"Yes." Sweep met Isin's gaze briefly over the woman's shoulder, ceding the fight to him.

Green turned and took an involuntary step backward. "Mr. Isin. Good. We need to talk."

He couldn't remember the last time anyone had called him *Mr.* Isin. After his time on *Sphinx* and *Vengeance,* the moniker sounded odd to his ear. "About what?"

She glanced between him and Sweep, her throat moving in a convulsive swallow.

He'd bet money she'd planned to speak with him alone, but her courage seemed to be failing her. Sweep's presence tended to make people feel safe. Isin often had the opposite effect.

She lifted her chin. "This is unacceptable." She gestured to the spacious cargo bay. "You cannot store my cargo here. Any member of your crew could come down here and steal it."

He barely suppressed a snort of laughter. She looked so earnest that he didn't want to make fun of her. He folded his arms over his chest. "And take it where? We'll be in space."

She glared at him. "I don't know. Anywhere! The point is, I'm paying you good money, and I expect better security than this. I don't want your crew pawing my cargo."

The top layer of enamel sheared off of Isin's molars. "The crew won't touch your cargo unless I order them to."

"How can you be sure?"

"Because the penalties for disobeying orders are... steep." He flicked his gaze toward the cargo bay door.

She followed his gaze and blinked, her dark eyes going round. But the effect didn't last long. She pulled her shoulders back. "Be that as it may, you must have a better option than... this." She swept her arms out to her sides.

Now she was insulting his ship. And her tone was grating on his nerves. He drew in a breath, focusing on how much she was paying him. "I might be able to offer an alternative if I knew what we'll be carrying."

Her face pinched as she considered her response. "It's part of my work."

"Which is?"

"Scientific research."

That was vague and unhelpful. "What type of research?"

"Nothing you'd understand."

That got his hackles up. He took a step forward, invading her personal space. "Don't let the scars fool you, *Ms. Green.*" He put emphasis on the Ms., although he was beginning to suspect he was dealing with *Dr.* Green. Or rather, Dr. Whoever She Was. "I graduated top of my class at Columbia. I assure you, I'm capable of understanding your little research project just fine."

She leaned away from him, her lips parting in surprise and her gaze darting to Sweep for support.

He gave her a cool stare. "Appearances can be deceiving."

She glanced back at Isin. "I'll keep that in mind." She took several slow breaths before lowering her voice to a near whisper. "I can't share any details. Suffice to say my research is very important. As is your... security."

At least her attitude had improved. He was used to people viewing him as a thug—he'd encouraged it. It allowed him to get the upper hand. But now she knew he had a brain, too. He stepped back. "What type of—*security*—did you have in mind?"

She propped her hands on her hips, her previous irritation reviving. "You tell me. You're the mercenary. Surely you have a vault. Or a safe. Or some other way to secure valuable cargo."

He did, but not one he'd admit to. Only three people knew about the half-meter-square safe built into the bulkhead in his cabin. Shash, because she'd designed and installed it, Sweep because he'd set the security, and Itorye because she knew all his secrets.

If what they picked up would fit in there, he'd consider making use of it. But until the cargo was onboard, that option was off the table. "I can assure you, whatever you entrust to me will be delivered safely to the destination."

"What if another ship attacks?"

Was she serious? He deadpanned his response. "We'll give them whatever they want."

Her jaw dropped. "*What?*"

Even Sweep looked at him strangely.

Was he the only person in the room with a sense of humor? He sighed. "I will defend this ship *and your cargo* with my life. You have my word."

She glowered. "The word of a mercenary."

He dropped his voice to a warning growl. "The word of a *captain.*" His gaze clashed with hers, daring her to challenge him.

She stared back without flinching.

He gave her points for that.

"Well then, *Captain,* I will hold you personally responsible if anything goes wrong." Dropping her gaze, she reached into a pocket of her jumpsuit and pulled out a data card and a mini tablet. She inserted the card into the tablet and turned the tablet toward Isin. "Place your thumb here." She indicated the tablet's flat surface.

He did as instructed, pressing the thumb of his right hand to the smooth glass.

"Now your forefinger."

He switched to his index finger.

They repeated the process with all five fingers before she pulled the tablet back. She tapped on the surface until the device made a soft beeping noise, then removed the data card and held it out. "The card has been calibrated to your fingerprints. You're the only one who will be able to access the contents."

Isin accepted the slim card. "What's on it?"

"The instructions for the pickup and delivery of the cargo."

"I'll review it before we leave."

"Don't bother."

The haughtiness in her tone raised his temperature a couple degrees. "Why not?"

"The card uses astrometric encoding for security. You will need to reach specific locations before you'll be able to access the information."

The figure she'd quoted for the job was starting to seem a little low. "Is that absolutely necessary?"

"Yes. I'll transmit your initial coordinates after we've departed Gallows Edge. From there, you'll be directed by the data on the card until we rendezvous at the final destination. The information contained on the card is for your eyes only. Share with your crew only what is absolutely necessary to complete your task."

She was treating him like a test subject in an elaborate lab experiment. Nothing about this plan sat well. "Does Natasha know about this?"

"It doesn't concern her."

He lifted a brow. "Everything about this job concerns her." And him. He'd make damn sure she knew about their client's manipulations before they left this rock. He held up the data card. "I could refuse to play your little game."

She lifted her chin. "And I could hire someone else."

He seriously doubted that. From the moment he'd spotted her talking to Natasha in the bar, he'd sensed a tremor of desperation, like a low-grade fever. She needed them. What he didn't know was why.

Her bravado seemed calculated to conceal her anxiety. And if he hadn't spent years studying the art of negotiation, he wouldn't have picked up on it. How long had she been waiting on Gallows Edge, hoping to find a crew willing to accept her offer?

If the final decision were his to make, he'd put her off the ship. But he and Natasha had agreed to take this job. Unless she changed her mind, he was stuck with Green's cloak and dagger routine. "Everything I'll need to know is on this card?"

"That's correct. And you must follow my instructions to the letter. No deviations."

"Why not?"

"If you fail to follow orders, you'll put your crew in danger."

He straightened, his fist closing around the card. "You said the cargo wasn't dangerous."

"It isn't. But the security surrounding it is."

"Is that why you didn't bring it to Gallows Edge?"

She waved the question away. "You'll find all the answers you need on the card."

Sure he would. Except the most important ones.

What the hell had he gotten himself into?

Eleven

"Green just paid me a visit." Isin paced the deck of his cabin.

"I know. She said she wanted to inspect your ship. One second." Natasha's voice grew fainter. "Move the cannons to the storage compartment on D deck."

"On it." Kenji's voice drifted over the comm in the background, followed by a muffled reply from Fleur.

Sounded like Natasha was supervising the storage of the new munitions for *Phoenix*.

"She refused to tell me where we're going."

"What?" He had her full attention now. "She didn't say anything about keeping that a secret."

"She claims it's a security issue. She gave me a data card with astrometric encoding. It will only unlock the information when we reach the right coordinates." His gaze settled on the panel that concealed the safe behind his bunk. "She also mentioned the cargo has a security system that could be hazardous."

Natasha grumbled something that was far from complimentary. "We'll just see about that." She closed the connection before he could respond.

He almost felt sorry for Green. When Natasha got her ruff up, she was a force to be reckoned with. But Green had instigated this little drama. How much of a threat did her secret pose to his ship and crew? Was the money worth the risk?

He opened a connection to Itorye. "Status report."

"Restocking of the armory is almost complete. Shash is still going over the engine checks. She's been grumbling about modifications Willow made to the inertial sequencer, but I don't expect it to cause a delay in our departure. Do we have a heading?"

"Not yet." He filled her in on his interaction with Green.

"Do you believe her claim regarding scientific study?"

"I'm not sure. Maybe. She certainly has the mind for it. But what would a scientist be doing on Gallows Edge?"

"Illegal research or experimentation?"

"There aren't any science facilities or technology hubs on this outpost. Why come *here*?"

"The Fleet doesn't."

"True." Which gave credence to Natasha's guess that she was hiding from the law. Not a big deal. Half his crew fit solidly into that category. But with the kind of money and security Green had invested in this job, whatever she was tangled up in was big. Going head-to-head with a Fleet ship wasn't on his agenda.

He rubbed a hand across his forehead, trying to relieve the tension at his temples. "This just got a lot more complicated."

His comm pinged with an incoming communication. "That's Natasha. I'll see you on the bridge in a few."

"Understood."

He switched channels. "What did she say?"

Natasha's voice poured through the connection with the heat of a lava flow. "That woman would try the patience of a saint! Not only did she stonewall me about our destination and the data card, she's insisting I ban all crewmembers from B deck for the duration of the flight. I told her what she could do with that plan." She sounded like she might be considering throwing her passenger overboard.

He'd been focusing on the obstacles Green had presented to him, but Natasha's trip was likely to be a lot more challenging than his. "Do you want to change your mind? Tell her to find someone else?"

"I'd love to, but no. I've flown with plenty of folks who irritated me more than she does."

He was willing to bet he was one of them.

"I can handle it. At least this one's paying well." Her exhale hissed over the line. "We'll stay together until we reach the jump window coordinates at the edge of the system. She said you'll be able to access the data on the card at that point. If there's anything we don't like about the situation, we'll scratch the plan and leave her at the next outpost we visit."

He couldn't decide which outcome to hope for—the boatload of money they stood to earn if they kept the job, or the satisfaction it would give him to dump Green at a random outpost. "Contact me as soon as you're ready to leave."

"Will do. I'd better go see what she's doing to my B deck cabins. Probably erecting a barricade." She closed the channel.

Isin stood still for a long moment, various *what if* scenarios running through his head. Green's insistence on secrecy didn't bother him nearly as much as the idea of separating *Vengeance* and *Phoenix*. The job might be benign, but the red flags were multiplying. He hated dealing with so many unknowns, especially if it put Natasha in danger.

At least he'd sent Kenji, Avril, and Fleur to join her crew. If they ran into any unpleasant circumstances, Avril and Fleur would defend the ship to their last breath. And Kenji had sworn to personally protect Natasha with his life. His oath was the only reason Isin had agreed to let her out of his sight.

Twelve

"We've reached the jump window coordinates." Byrd, *Vengeance*'s pilot, rotated his chair to face the captain's platform on the bridge. "What now?"

Isin glanced at the bridgescreen image of the *Phoenix* off their starboard side. "Hold here."

Byrd settled into his chair and stretched out his long legs, like he was preparing for a nap. "Gladly." The kid had whined about the lack of R&R while they were on Gallows Edge, earning a sharp rebuke. Not that Isin expected much maturity from the twenty-three-year-old. He'd kept him on after the coup because of his piloting skills, not his attitude.

Isin glanced at Itorye, seated at the tactical station to his right. "You have the bridge."

"Aye."

She moved to the captain's platform as he headed for the small bridge compartment that housed a utilitarian workstation and chair. After the door shut behind him, he dropped into the chair, pulled the data card from his pocket, and slid it into the card reader, placing his hand on the scanner until the reader confirmed authorization.

Green's face appeared on the monitor mounted into the bulkhead above the desk. The background image was non-descript, like she'd recorded the message while stuffed into a closet. "Before I go into any details regarding your assignment, I must impress upon you the importance of your discretion, and the necessity for following my instructions to the letter. Failure to do so could pose a serious danger to you and your crew."

"So you said," Isin muttered.

"I am holding you personally responsible for keeping the cargo safe after it is onboard your ship. Proceed to the following coordinates."

He paused the playback and pulled up a star chart. The coordinates she'd given would place them in a system seven light years away. According to the database, the system didn't have any habitable planets or moons. He resumed playback.

"Once there, you will receive additional instructions. Do not deviate from the course that has been laid out, and do not contact the *Phoenix*. Maintain a communications blackout at all times. I will have the remainder of your payment ready when you reach the rendezvous point."

The screen went blank.

Isin leaned back in his chair, running his forefinger along the ridge of his scar as he stared at the screen. He'd received more cryptic orders before, but never in a situation where he was flying blind. Or where he was being asked to cut communications with half his crew.

Which brought him to his next task. He opened a comm channel to Natasha.

She responded without preamble. "Do you have your instructions?"

"Yes."

"And?" she prompted when he didn't continue.

"And... she's keeping us on a very tight leash. I think she's seriously paranoid about being followed. She demanded a communications blackout."

Natasha snorted. "Yeah, you can ignore that. She and I already had a little chat."

"What did you say?"

"That if that was one of her conditions, she could walk back to Gallows Edge."

The corner of his lip lifted. "I'm sorry I missed that."

"Yeah, well, she's an idiot if she wants to split us up and then enforce a blackout. I simply made her aware of that fact. Eventually she saw it my way."

Having been on the receiving end of Natasha's ire on many occasions, he could picture the scene easily. "So we're good to go?"

"Unless you have any objections."

"Oh, I have objections. But she's paying to override them. And you're the one who has to deal with her until the rendezvous."

"Don't remind me. Hopefully she'll still be alive to pay us when we reach our destination." A beat of silence passed. "Be safe."

The simple words flowed over him like ice melt and sunshine, triggering alternating patches of heat and cold. On the rare occasions when Natasha treated him like a friend, his mind and body couldn't seem to agree on how to react.

The sunshine must have won, because he responded before he'd decided what to say. "You too, Natasha."

Thirteen

Hours later, Isin stepped onto the bridge and found Byrd slouched at the navigation console, a gaming visor covering the top half of his face. The mottled image on the bridgescreen indicated they were still in their interstellar jump.

Isin slipped up beside him and latched a hand onto his shoulder.

Byrd let out a yip like a startled dog, his head swinging around although he wouldn't be able to see through the visor.

"Having fun?" Isin kept his tone conversational. Technically Byrd wasn't breaking any of the ship's rules by playing games at his station, but it rankled nonetheless.

Byrd used his free arm to pull the device off his head. "I was until you interrupted. My avatar just took a hit because of you." The irritation in Byrd's eyes matched his scowl.

Isin leaned down so they were nose to nose. "Would *you* like to take a hit from *me*?"

The scowl disappeared as color leeched from Byrd's cheeks. "No."

"Good. Then get me the ETA to our destination."

He released his grip and stepped up to the captain's chair while Byrd scrambled to pull up the information.

The kid had raw talent and a steady hand at the controls, but he could be erratic and undisciplined. He was also convinced of his own invulnerability. He treated piloting *Vengeance* like an elaborate game without consequences.

Isin couldn't help contrasting the young pilot with Natasha. They probably weren't that far apart in age, but they were like night and day. She had a firm grasp on her own mortality and understood how her actions affected the entire crew. It was one of the qualities that made her an exceptional pilot. She took risks just as Byrd did, but she knew the dangers and saw the big picture. Byrd saw only the tiny square that directly affected him.

Convincing Natasha to take the job he'd offered her as pilot and captain of *Phoenix* would serve multiple purposes, including providing a wonderful mentor and role model for Byrd. If anyone could show him the error of his ways, it was Natasha.

"Twelve minutes to the system." Byrd stared straight ahead as he delivered the information.

"Where will the jump window put us in relation to the planets?"

"Halfway between the orbits of the fourth and fifth planets."

"Will either planet be close by?"

"Nope. They're currently on the opposite side of the star."

Not what he'd expected. Why would Green give them coordinates that put them in the middle of open space? "Any asteroids in the area?"

Byrd scanned the information on the console. "Nothing on the charts."

Reason enough to proceed with caution. "Calculate an exit jump that will take us to a nearby system. I want to be able to leave in a hurry if we run into unexpected complications."

"What complications?" Sweep asked from behind him.

Isin glanced over his shoulder as Sweep strode from the back hatch to the weapons and security console. "We're entering open space."

"Hmm." Sweep opened a comm channel. "Shorty, load torpedoes fore and aft and send Downey and Saddle to the guns."

"Aye."

Sweep met Isin's gaze. "Just in case."

Isin nodded. He trusted Sweep's judgment implicitly. While he'd honed his physical combat skills to a razor's edge in the past year, his knowledge of battle tactics were still rudimentary. Thankfully Sweep was a walking encyclopedia on the subject.

Itorye's heels clicked on the deck as she appeared at the forward hatch. She glanced at the bridgescreen before heading to her station. "Problem?" she asked as she settled into her chair and pivoted to face him.

He didn't question her timely arrival. Itorye monitored all shipboard communications, even during her off hours, keeping in touch with everything that happened on the ship. He didn't know how she routed all channels to her comm, and he didn't care. She kept the ship running smoothly. That's what mattered.

He filled her in on the situation. "As soon as we're clear of the jump, we need to scan for any ships or technology in the system."

"Understood."

Isin pulled up the ship's aft camera feed on the smaller monitor attached to his chair, angling it so he could see the image in his peripheral vision while keeping his focus on the front screen.

He waited with the others in silence, the rumble of the interstellar engines the only sound.

"Exiting the jump in five, four, three..." Byrd counted down until the interstellar engines gave way to the main engines and the bridgescreen filled with the inky black of the starfield.

Isin's fingers tightened on the armrests as his gaze swept from the monitor to the bridgescreen. He pivoted his chair in a quick one-hundred-eighty-degree turn, taking in as much of the visual field as possible. No ships waiting to strike. Only empty space and the system's star glowing like a penlight in the distance.

"No ships or other technology showing on scans," Itorye said.

"All clear," Sweep confirmed.

The tension in his chest eased a bit. "Hold position and stay alert."

He left the captain's platform and strode to the bridge compartment. As soon as the door closed behind him, he removed the data card Green had given him and inserted it in the card reader. Sure enough, a message appeared on the monitor, this time in text rather than a video. It provided a new set of coordinates, but not in this system.

He blew out a breath. Their client's paranoia was getting on his nerves. Apparently she planned to have them hop around like rabbits for a while before revealing the pickup location for their cargo.

And poor Natasha had that woman on her ship. He could only imagine the challenges Green was throwing her way. Hopefully she would arrive at their destination with her sanity intact.

He sent the coordinates to Byrd before retrieving the card and stalking back onto the bridge. "Byrd, take us to the new coordinates."

Itorye lifted one slender brow.

"I'll explain later," he grumbled as he sank into the captain's chair.

The starfield pivoted on the bridgescreen as Byrd altered their trajectory, taking the ship to their new jump window.

Isin counted out the minutes by visualizing a trail of money. Every kilometer they traveled brought him closer to that goal. He had to remember that.

Not helping. His teeth still ground together, making a muscle in his jaw pop. He needed a different kind of distraction.

As soon as the interstellar engines kicked in, he turned to Sweep. "How about a round in the Cage?"

Sweep's eyes gleamed with the light of battle. "Looking for some fresh bruises?"

"Looking to give a few."

"You're on."

Fourteen

A swollen jaw and two interstellar jumps later, the infernal data card finally announced they'd reached their destination, a system of five planets surrounding a red dwarf star.

Isin's boots crunched on the hard-packed snow of the ice moon orbiting the third planet, though he barely heard the sound through his military-grade spacesuit. The frozen tundra visible through his helmet wasn't much to look at either, an expanse of white broken by jutting grey rock formations.

The cargo was somewhere on this moon, although the ship's scanners had failed to pick up any signs of life or technology. He was using a mobile reader attached to his suit to access the real-time data the card was providing.

The system's dwarf star was directly overhead, but its low luminosity cast the surroundings in a faint glow, making it feel more like twilight than midday. Itorye walked through the swirling snow on his right, her suit giving her lean body a slightly more padded silhouette, while Shash strode along on his left, outfitted in a custom suit she'd designed and constructed herself. It conformed to her curves in a way that made him wonder how it could possibly be insulating her from the frigid temperatures.

The data card had specified three people were required to obtain the cargo—no more, no less. After the way Green had emphasized the hazards that would arise if he failed to follow orders to the letter, he'd decided a larger contingent would be unwise. Itorye had landed the

Dagger a quarter of a kilometer to the east and, per the instructions, they'd set out on foot.

He compared the information from the data card to the sensor readings displayed on the faceplate of his helmet. Another two hundred meters at least. He peered through the gloom. Was that a rocky outcropping up ahead? It was hard to make out anything distinct through the dim light and blowing snow, but the distance seemed about right.

Shash's voice came through his helmet comm. "Any idea what we're looking for?"

He'd expected the card to provide full details after they'd landed, but so far he'd only been given a direction and distance to location. The next time he was face to face with Green, he intended to tell her exactly what he thought of her little hide and seek operation. "Not yet. But we're getting close."

"I don't know why we had to land so far away. There's plenty of room for a transport here."

She was right. They were walking across an open expanse of flat land. Nothing about the area would have prevented the *Dagger* from landing, a fact that ratcheted Isin's tension up another notch. Everything about this scenario screamed danger. Which is why all three of them were heavily armed.

But nothing moved except the snow as they plodded through the monotonous sea of white, the dark silhouette he'd spotted in the distance growing into a rocky promontory reaching toward the sky.

The wind died down as they approached the lee of the stony mass, and a new message appeared on his display. "There's a cave entrance over there."

He pointed to the right, leading the way around the collection of boulders at the base, pushing through larger drifts of snow until a natural opening appeared in the rock. The dim illumination from the red dwarf didn't touch the pitch blackness that lay in a puddle a couple meters in.

"Lights." Isin switched on the headlamps for his suit, directing the beams into the opening. The tunnel curved down and to the right, the floor sloping at a five-degree angle. He stepped inside, the subtle whir of the snowstorm muffled in the enclosed space. He didn't have much clearance for walking—the cave was only about two-and-a-half meters tall, and about half as wide. If the cargo was inside, it couldn't be very large.

He checked the sensor readings, but couldn't pick up any signals through the surrounding rock. No new information from the data card, either. Great. Nothing like going into an enclosed space blind. Unstrapping his rifle, he started down the decline. "Stay close."

The narrow passage wouldn't allow them to walk side by side in their suits, especially with weapons at the ready, so Shash followed behind him, with Itorye bringing up the rear.

The tunnel continued on a fairly straight line for fifteen meters before curving sharply to the right and terminating at a small cavern roughly the size of *Vengeance*'s bridge. The ceiling rose to five meters at the center, giving the interior of the cavern the shape of an overturned bowl. A rectangular metal shipping crate sat against the far wall.

He paused just inside the entrance as Shash and Itorye stepped up beside him. Data appeared on his faceplate. "A security field just activated across the center of the cavern." He picked up a pebble from the ground and tossed it through the air in the direction of the metal crate.

A sizzle and pop accompanied a flash of light as the pebble struck the energy field and exploded.

"Friendly," Shash muttered.

"Friendlier than the alternative." He lifted his gaze to the ceiling, where two compact auto-cannons were aimed at the entrance. "According to the info on the data card, if more than three of us had entered, those would have fired instead." A fact the data card had kept secret until they'd crossed the threshold.

Shash harrumphed, sounding more impressed than irritated. Then again, she'd never met Green.

He scanned the cavern with his lamp, illuminating a discreet unit attached to the rock wall to their left. "That must be the control box."

Shash took a step toward it and halted, glancing over her shoulder at him. "Your little card have any objection to my going over there?"

"No." He holstered his rifle and turned to Itorye. "Keep your eyes open."

She nodded, taking up a position at the entrance to the cavern, her weapon at the ready.

He followed Shash along the curve of the wall to the control box.

She crouched, bringing the box to eye level. "It's a standard G-form security regulator, but juiced to produce a much stronger field. It requires a six digit code to deactivate."

"Which I have."

"Great. What is it?"

He placed a hand on her shoulder as she reached toward the box. "Wait. The unit has been attached to a bio sensor rigged with an explosive device." The warning flashing on his faceplate made his core temperature rise a few degrees. "To turn off the security without triggering an explosion, you'll have to remain within half a meter of the device after you enter the code."

Shash pivoted to face him. "And what happens when I eventually have to move? I'm not planning to become a permanent resident."

He reread through the information from the card. "It doesn't say."

Shash let loose with a particularly colorful phrase. "This is ridiculous! Why don't I just disable this thing? I could—"

"No. Green said if we followed the instructions to the letter, we'd be fine. If you attempt to disable the device, it could blow the entire cavern."

Shash didn't say anything, but the look she shot him indicated he'd just insulted her engineering skills.

Too bad. His only concern was getting the cargo onboard as quickly as possible. The sooner they got off this moon, the sooner he could meet up with Natasha and get paid. Then he'd never have to deal with Green and her paranoia again.

He held Shash's gaze. "We follow the instructions. Understood?"

Her mouth twisted like she was sucking on a lemon. "Yeah."

The setup explained why retrieving the cargo required at least two people. He glanced at the metal crate. What trick would he and Itorye have to pull off to penetrate the next level of defense?

Shash entered the code as he recited it. The unit beeped and the red light turned green.

At the same moment, a new message appeared on his faceplate. "Field's down." He picked up another pebble and tossed it just to be sure. It landed with a soft plop near the metal crate. "Itorye, you're with me."

She joined him as he approached the crate. It was almost two meters wide and three meters long, too large to fit through the tunnel. That meant it had been assembled inside the cavern. The card's instructions directed him to a panel embedded in the center of one of the crate's longer sides. The display lit up when he stepped in front of it.

The words *Enter Authorization Code* appeared on the screen, along with a digital keypad.

The data card supplied another six digit number.

Isin flexed his fingers before typing in the code.

Access Granted.

More instructions from the data card appeared. He glanced at Itorye after reading through them. "Look for an indentation on the left side at the corner just below the top seam."

She ran her hand along the top of the crate as he crouched by the opposite corner and sought out an indentation on the bottom seam. After he located it, he reread the instructions. "We have to press both at the same time to release the locks." Which would be impossible for one person to do given the size of the crate and the location of the release points. Green had specified exactly three people for this job. Now he knew why.

"Found it."

"On three. One... two... three."

A soft whirring sound reached him from inside the crate and the seal broke, the lid popping open as the pressure from the interior forced its way out.

Itorye gripped the hinged lid in one hand, lifting it until it settled against the wall of the cavern. She peered into the crate. "Not what I'd expected."

Isin rose, catching sight of the object within. *Not at all.*

He'd considered countless possibilities for this escapade, all of which involved fairly large, valuable objects. But the opaque cube sitting in the exact center of the crate was small enough that he could tuck it under his arm.

He checked his helmet display for instructions, but none appeared. Reaching inside the crate, he picked up the cube. It came easily, weighing no more than his suit's helmet. The unmarked surface reminded him of a block carved from a glacier—frosted blue-white, smooth sides, no discernable way to access whatever was inside. And he had to believe *something* was inside. The cube itself couldn't possibly be valuable enough to require all the cloak and dagger security Green had set up. It was unremarkable, something that would be dismissed as irrelevant if it was sitting on a desk or shelf.

Which might be the point. Green had claimed the object wasn't dangerous to his ship or crew. Looking at it now, he wasn't sure whether he believed her. Its nondescript nature felt too contrived.

But it was his job to deliver it. He met Itorye's gaze. "Let's get out of here."

Itorye strode toward the entrance while Isin headed for Shash. As soon as he crossed the beam that marked the security line in the center of the cavern, a new message appeared on his faceplate. *You have thirty seconds to reach the surface.*

The display switched to two large digits. *30... 29... 28...*

Adrenaline poured into his veins. He reached Shash in a heartbeat, grabbing her by the arm and thrusting her toward the cavern's entrance. "*Run!*"

She moved like lightning, darting into the tunnel after Itorye. He followed close on her heels, the ominous countdown moving in time with the pumping of his legs in the padded spacesuit. He wrapped the cube in his arms as he sprinted up the tunnel. The light from their suits splashed across the rocks, creating a visual cacophony that threatened to throw off his balance.

15... 14... 13....

He rounded the curve that opened to the hazy white of the snowstorm. Itorye stood like a sentinel outside, waiting for them.

9... 8... 7....

"Get clear!" he shouted as he and Shash raced onto the hard-packed snow. His boots skidded on the surface and he went down to one knee, the cube digging into his ribcage and forcing air from his lungs. As he lurched to his feet, a tremor shook the ground. A plume of rock shot into the air to his left, the chunks falling towards him like deadly raindrops.

He stumbled back, his boots continuing to slide as he tried to reach his rifle.

Before he could get a grip, the nearest projectiles exploded in a shower of sparks amid the whine of weapons fire from Itorye and Shash. They stood side by side, casually picking off the larger chunks as easily as a child popped soap bubbles.

As soon as the last stragglers had been vaporized, Itorye holstered her weapon and faced him. "Any damage to your suit?"

"No. You?" He glanced between her and Shash.

They both shook their heads.

No thanks to Green and her data card. What psychopathic person set a thirty-second timer to destroy an empty cavern on a barren moon? Was his crew supposed to fail? To die in the attempt? One thing was for sure. He'd be asking her when he saw her. And tacking on a hefty surcharge to his fee.

Fifteen

"What do you think it is?" Itorye sat with her elbows propped on the small desk in Isin's cabin, her chin resting on her folded hands as she gazed at the cube.

"I have no idea." Not that he hadn't given the matter considerable thought during the return hike to the *Dagger* and the flight back to *Vengeance*. He'd only reached one conclusion—he'd be stowing the cube in his cabin's safe. He didn't want such a small and potentially valuable item to wander off. Or accidentally blow a hole in his ship.

The safe had been constructed of materials designed to protect the contents even if the ship was destroyed. Nothing short of a nuclear blast, from within or without, would open the safe.

Shash and Itorye had run interference for him, assigning the crew tasks that kept them out of his path, as he transported the cube from the shuttle bay to his cabin. The data card had conveyed a new set of coordinates when he'd inserted it into the reader on his desk, and he'd relayed the information to Sweep and Byrd on the bridge. The ship was already underway.

He settled into the foldout chair opposite her. "Do you have any theories about what it is?"

"Possibly." Her gaze traced over the cube's surface. "It certainly wasn't designed for use by the Fleet."

"How can you be sure?"

She lifted her gaze and raised one perfectly shaped brow.

He grunted. "Never mind." Itorye had once told him her father held a powerful position in the Galactic Fleet's science and engineering sector. If she said the cube wasn't a Fleet design, she was right. "So it's corporate?"

"Uh-huh. Most likely a well-funded research project."

"That would fit with what Green told us."

"You sound surprised."

He shrugged. "After all the runaround, I was beginning to think the entire setup was a ruse."

A smile played across Itorye's lips. "It was planned out the way a scientist would create security."

"Or the way a scientist would set a trap."

"Perhaps." Itorye slipped a handheld scanner from her pocket and held it up. "Do you mind?" She gestured to the cube.

"Go right ahead." The more they knew about their strange cargo, the better.

Itorye passed the device in front of the cube, pausing to check the readings before continuing over the top and sides. "Fascinating."

"What?"

"I'm not getting any readings."

"There's nothing inside?"

She shook her head. "I mean the material used for the exterior casing is repelling or distorting all attempts at scanning." She pivoted the scanner so he could see the data. Or rather, lack of data.

"Any idea what it's made of?"

"Something synthetic, but without any readings, it's impossible to say what." She set down the scanner and ran the pads of her fingers over the top of the cube. "Or what's inside."

"Green said it didn't pose a danger to the crew."

"Do you believe her?"

"Whether I do or not, I'm not taking any chances." Scooping the cube off the table, he walked the few steps to his bunk, set the cube on the mattress, and detached the false panel that hid the safe. After entering the code to unlock it, he pulled open the door and deposited the cube inside. "It can stay in here until we reach our destination." He closed the door and sealed it, then replaced the false panel.

"Do you think she stole it?"

He'd considered that question, too. "If she did, why would she go through such elaborate measures to distance herself from it? Although she does seem convinced someone will attempt to take it from her."

"True." Itorye rose from her seat. "I assume you'll want to increase security while we're en route to the rendezvous point?"

He nodded. "Have Sweep draw up a crew rotation so we'll have continual monitoring of tactical data and overlapping shifts for the gunner stations. We don't want any surprises."

Sixteen

Another uninhabited system. Another pointless stop, just like all the other systems they'd seen during this trip.

The beginnings of a headache pushed at Isin's temples. They appeared to be on another zigzag route that would eventually lead to their destination, whatever that was. Green had indicated the job would take two weeks. It had only been eight days since they'd left Gallows Edge.

The pointless hopping around was trying his patience. It didn't help that he was now carrying a mysterious cube of unknown origin and content. Nothing about this scenario sat right.

Sweep had agreed, which is why they'd scouted out all the neighboring systems and made contingency plans based on every scenario they could conjure of how this might play out, including the possibility that someone might try to steal the cube before they reached their destination. Maybe even the cube's legitimate owner.

Itorye glanced over from the tactical console. "A message came in for you from the *Phoenix*."

He was out of the captain's chair in a nanosecond. "Byrd, take us to the new coordinates. I'll be in my cabin."

Exiting the bridge through the forward hatch, he reached his cabin in six long strides. He sat at his desk, calling up the encrypted vid message on his monitor before his cabin door swung closed behind him.

Natasha's image appeared on the screen. She was seated in the pilot's chair on *Phoenix*'s bridge, her duster flaring out like a cloak. The background lighting was subdued, indicating the night cycle.

She crossed her arms over her chest and let out a gusty sigh. "I'm beginning to regret taking this job."

His lips quirked up. At least they agreed on that.

"Not only has Green commandeered B deck, but she refuses to tell me our final destination. Instead of a straight shot, she has us hopping around from system to system like a rabbit evading a fox." She made a face.

Another shared experience.

"We seem to be heading in the general direction of Osiris, so maybe that's where we'll end up meeting you, but if that's the case, the route we're taking is ludicrous."

Osiris? That wasn't the direction *Vengeance* was heading, although they weren't exactly moving away from it either.

He paused the playback. He could ignore the data card and tell Byrd to plot a course to Osiris, but arriving at the outer rim planet ahead of *Phoenix* wouldn't help his cause, since Green wouldn't be there to take the cube off his hands. Better to follow her bunny trail than sit like a target in orbit.

He resumed the playback.

Natasha's voice dropped to a low growl. "I just hope we get where we're going before I strangle her. Marlin spent half the day making a fabulous vegetable lasagna from scratch, and she had the gall to complain it was too spicy. Too spicy! The man is a *master* with spices. The food was perfect. She turned up her nose at the ginger snaps he'd baked, too."

Isin's brows lifted. Marlin was a good cook—the entire crew had benefitted from his efforts while they'd been onboard *Phoenix*. Too bad for Green if she couldn't appreciate that fact.

Natasha glanced over her shoulder at the bridge hatch, which led to the lower decks. "Marlin will handle her, though." Her pale aqua eyes sparkled with mischief as she leaned closer to the camera. "I have a feeling she'll be getting dry toast and water for breakfast tomorrow."

The beginnings of a smile pulled at his mouth. If Green wasn't careful, Natasha would probably make sure that was her only option for the rest of the trip.

"Kenji's keeping Fleur and Avril busy upgrading the ship's weapons system. Pete's helping when he has time. Now that the armory is cleaned and restocked, they're determined to get the new cannons installed. Kenji also requested thirty minutes for target practice when we reach the next system to fine tune the calibrations on the torpedo launchers." Her smile looked smug. "That'll shake up our passenger a bit."

And insure *Phoenix* would be ready for action by the time the ship reached the rendezvous point.

"That's it for us. I hope you're having an easier time with the cargo than I'm having with our client. She's still arguing for a communications blackout, but she's not winning that one. Besides, she has to sleep sometime." She brought her hand over her mouth, stifling a yawn. "And so do I. Kenji'll be here in a few minutes to relieve me, so I'll wrap this up. Let me know if you acquired the cargo yet, and if you seem to be headed for Osiris, too."

The screen went black.

He gazed at it for several minutes, parsing what she'd said for clues that might help him solve the mystery of the cube. But other than the possibility of their final destination being Osiris, she hadn't given him anything more to go on regarding his mysterious cargo.

He switched on his vid camera and started recording. "We've secured the cargo, although I couldn't tell you what it is even if I wanted to. It's encased in a cube that has resisted efforts to scan the contents." Although he hadn't given up yet. Shash had asked to take a look at it during her next off-duty cycle. She might be able to shed some light on the subject.

"We're system hopping, too. The data card only provides information on a need to know basis. It's hard to say if we'll end up at Osiris or not. Green has a knack for creating... unnecessary complications." He grimaced. "I'm beginning to feel like a subject in one of her research experiments." Which he could very well be, come to think of it. The idea hadn't occurred to him before, but this entire job could be an elaborate behavioral or social study. The possibility didn't improve his mood.

"The system we're heading for is uninhabited, as were the others we've passed through. Based on the timetable Green gave us, I'm expecting another few hops before we reach our final destination." That day couldn't get here fast enough. "In the future, I plan to avoid working for paranoid scientists. Tell Kenji I expect a full report on the new weapons installation when we see you. Isin out."

Seventeen

Isin rotated the captain's chair to take in the three-hundred-sixty-degree image on the bridgescreen. The star at the center of the system shone as a distant point of light as *Vengeance* passed the outermost planet on the way to the coordinates provided by the data card. "Let me guess. No habitable planets and no ships."

Itorye glanced over from her station. "Correct."

The routine was becoming irritatingly familiar. Arrive in the system, go to the coordinates in the middle of nowhere, receive new instructions from the data card. He drummed his fingers on the armrest because he couldn't do anything else until they reached the coordinates.

The data card was tucked in his pocket. He'd come to loathe the thing, but whenever they entered a new system, he was forced to carry it like a miniature anchor. His palms itched to take action, but the damn card held him immobile.

The minutes crept by as Byrd guided the ship closer to the star, the silence on the bridge becoming more oppressive with each breath.

They passed the fifth planet, a gas giant twice the size of Jupiter, and a cluster of orbiting moons.

As the planet retreated into the distance, Byrd pivoted in his chair to face Isin. "We've reached the coordinates."

"All stop."

The image on the screen froze as the ship's forward motion ceased.

"Anything on comm or sensors?"

"No." Itorye's voice didn't change inflection, but he could tell she'd grown weary of Green's little game, too.

He pushed out of his chair. "Be right back."

Stalking into the bridge compartment, he shoved the data card into the reader and waited for it to verify his fingerprints. He didn't even bother sitting down. He'd been through this song and dance one too many times.

Sure enough, a message popped onto the display—another set of coordinates. He checked the star charts before removing the card, confirming the destination would land them in another uninhabited system. He ground his molars together, but what could he do? Maybe this would be the last detour. They were only three days from the two week mark. And this location would bring them closer to Osiris.

Returning to the bridge, he gave the coordinates to Byrd. "Lay in a course and get us out of here."

"On it." He sounded as tired of the monotony as the rest of them.

The bridgescreen image shifted as *Vengeance* banked, heading out of the system.

"Let me know when—" A jolt threw him off balance, sending him sprawling against the security station. He grabbed onto the edge of the console, his gaze meeting Sweep's. "Did something hit us?" he barked as the shriek of alarms filled the air and more tremors rocked the ship.

"No."

"Then what the hell's happening?"

"An explosion in the engine room."

"All stop," he called out to Byrd. But the vibration of the engines had already ceased. So had the tremors. He strode to the captain's chair and opened a comm channel. "Shash! What's going on?"

It took a moment before she replied. When she did, the blare of the alarms and background noise in the engine room made it difficult to hear her. "I don't know! The engine just blew."

He didn't like the sound of that. "I'll be right there."

Exiting through the back hatch, he vaulted down the five stairs that led to the engine room opening at the end of the passageway. The acrid smell of scorched insulation and metal wiring reached him first, followed by the haze of smoke pouring out of the main compartment. Shash's shouted commands guided him to his destination.

"I'm closing off the compartment! Get clear!"

Willow darted out of the side compartment as a klaxon sounded and the firewalls came down, while Pine operated a handheld fire extinguisher, coating the sparks that leapt through the gap as it closed. Shash stood hunched over the main console. "Cutting primary power." The lights flickered and went out, replaced by the reddish-yellow glow of the emergency lighting. The alarms silenced too.

He stopped beside her, his ears still ringing from the cacophony. "What's our status?"

She kept her focus on the panel, the patterned glow from the controls creating eerie shadows on her face in the low lighting. "We've got a level four fire in the main engine compartment. I've cut power so we can get containment." She tapped in a command to initialize the fire suppression system. The data on the console indicated the compartment's emergency hatch had opened to the fire tube that led to the exterior, venting the oxygen into space and taking the fire with it.

As soon as the panel flashed green, she closed the emergency hatch. "It's out. Closing the seal and re-pressurizing the compartment." A faint clank and hiss followed as the system obeyed her command. She stared at the firewall, her jaw clenching.

Not a good sign. "What caused this?"

She finally looked at him, the emergency lighting painting her face in shades of red, her eyes glowing in the darkness. Her voice rumbled with thinly concealed anger. "I went over every millimeter of this system while we were on Gallows Edge. Everything was in perfect working order. An explosion like this—" She gestured at the sealed compartment. "It doesn't just happen. Not on my watch."

Her implication settled on his shoulders like a small moon. Something was rotten in Demark. And they were stranded in the middle of nowhere. "How soon can you get the engines back online?"

Her lips peeled back from her teeth in a grim smile. "Depends on the damage. Main engines? A day, maybe two. But interstellar engines? Could be a week or more."

A week. If she was correct, they didn't have that kind of time to spare. "What about shields and weapons?"

"They're down, too, but I might be able to get partial restoration with auxiliary power."

"Do it. Then focus on the main engines. We need to be mobile as quickly as possible."

Shash gave a curt nod.

He leaned closer, his voice a low growl. "And I want to know who did this."

Eighteen

Isin sat in front of the vid recorder in his cabin, his hands curled into fists. He'd held off making this recording until after Shash's initial report had come in. They wouldn't have power to the main engines for eighteen hours. And interstellar engines would take another four days, minimum.

They'd be behind schedule for the rendezvous with Green, but that didn't bother him. Green could wait for all he cared. No, he had to warn Natasha that he had a saboteur onboard.

Shash had confirmed the explosion was no accident. She was still investigating the root cause, but the pattern of destruction was too precise and effective at crippling *Vengeance* to have been random. She'd sealed off the engine room with a security code to keep anyone from tampering further.

He'd placed all personnel on lockdown in their quarters under the guise that the explosion had caused a potentially lethal leak that had to be isolated and repaired. In addition to Shash, only Itorye, Sweep, Jake, and Byrd were free to move about the ship. He'd stationed Byrd on the bridge to monitor for incoming vessels while Sweep worked on restoring power to weapons and shields. Jake was visiting every crewmember in their cabins, making a show of checking them for early signs of contamination to give credence to Isin's ruse, and treating the wounds Pine and Willow had sustained during the explosion. Itorye was assisting Shash with repairs in the damaged engine room compartment, and analyzing the debris for clues to their saboteur's identity. With mutiny on the table, the rest of the crew had become more of a threat than an asset.

His temples throbbed, probably because he'd been grinding his teeth for the past hour, waiting for Shash's report.

Taking a deep breath, he turned on the recorder and dove in without preamble. "We have a problem." He gave a brief outline of the situation, including their current coordinates—Green's restrictions be damned. "Shash'll get us moving as quickly as she can, but we're going to be late to the rendezvous point unless you can convince Green to tell us where we're going. I don't know if the sabotage is connected to Green or not. It could just be a power grab." Like the one he'd staged to overthrow Shim.

But whomever was hunting Green had to be at least as resourceful as she was, and as wealthy. He had to entertain the possibility that they'd figured out a way to contact a member of his crew, bribing them into sabotaging the ship.

If Green was on *Vengeance*, he could ask her, find out who was after her and what kind of force they could bring to the table. Instead, he'd need Natasha's help. "Convince Green to give us details about this cargo—what it is, who's after it, and anything else that would help us defend ourselves if her pursuers show up."

Pushing the words past his lips took considerable effort. Asking for help wasn't his style. And knowing that someone on his crew was colluding to disable the ship pushed his temper to the red line. "Get her to see reason. Send a reply as soon as you can. I'll be monitoring the comm."

He turned off the recorder and sent the message before leaving his cabin.

He didn't envy Natasha the task he'd given her. Green would have a lot to say when she heard the news. It wouldn't be a pleasant conversation. She was difficult in the best of circumstances. With her paranoid delusions potentially bearing fruit, she might go off the deep end.

But Natasha might enjoy the challenge. She certainly rose to the occasion whenever she debated with him. He just wished she wasn't having to save his sorry ass... again.

Nineteen

"Someone on this ship is getting spaced." Shash's growl accompanied a look that could cut glass. Her fingers curled into claws where they rested on the engine room console.

Isin exchanged a look with Itorye before returning his attention to Shash. "Tell me."

"Remote detonation of an S-line device that tore open the coolant conduits. The engines superheated when they were engaged, triggering the explosion that crippled the system." She pulled what looked like a piece of shrapnel out of her pocket and slapped it down on the console. "That's what's left of the device. To create the scope of damage this caused, the device had to go off shortly after we reengaged the engines. Any sooner and there wouldn't have been enough heat. Any later, and the explosion would have ripped a hole in the ship's hull."

"We have a smart saboteur." Itorye's dark eyes held an arctic chill. "They didn't want to seriously damage the ship."

"Which spells mutiny," Shash spat.

"Maybe." Isin appreciated her indignation on his behalf. "Or this could be tied to Green. The saboteur may not have wanted to risk damaging the cargo."

Shash snorted. "Great. We could get attacked on two fronts. Wouldn't that be fun."

Itorye turned to Isin. "Any word from *Phoenix?*"

"No, but depending on their location, it could take a while for Natasha to respond." He'd lost track of the number of times he'd checked his comm in the last couple hours.

They needed to identify the saboteur quickly, and one clue leapt out at him. "Who has the technical skill to bypass the system sensors and install that device?"

Shash's eyes widened a fraction before narrowing to slits. "Not many. Ranger, Willow, Camp. Maybe Pine."

"That shortens the list."

Itorye leaned a hip against the console. "Unless we're dealing with more than one person."

"I only need one." He wouldn't hesitate to use the Cage to get information out of whoever had done this to his ship.

Itorye gave a subtle nod of understanding.

"I want you two to focus on restoring power to main engines. Do whatever it takes to get us moving. Hotwire it if you have to."

Shash grimaced. "Oh, joy."

He continued as if she hadn't spoken. "I'll be in the infirmary with Jake, having a chat with our suspects." His lips lifted in a mirthless smile. "Turns out they've all tested positive for dangerous levels of radiation. I'm very concerned they won't survive."

Twenty

Jake sat at the built-in desk in the infirmary, making notes on his data pad as Pine exited the room.

As soon as the doors closed, Isin touched the control pad, locking the entrance to prevent anyone from entering. "Well?"

Jake looked up. "It's Camp."

Bingo. Jake had just confirmed Isin's assessment. "How could you tell?"

Jake's expression was unusually grim. "His eyes. The pupils dilated every time he lied."

Leave it to Jake to notice a tiny physiological change.

"I also detected traces on his skin of the chemical compound Shash said was used in the explosive device. The man doesn't scrub up well."

"I'm not sure he scrubs up at all." Camp's lack of hygiene had never been an issue. He was a good fighter and engineer. That was all that had mattered. Until now.

Jake stood, bringing him eye-level with Isin. "How did you figure it out?"

"The pattern of his responses." Camp had been far too calm, especially compared to the other three.

Willow had been nervous, fidgeting while Jake ran the scanner over her body, her gaze darting from him to Isin, a slight tremor in her voice when she'd asked if she was going to get sick. As soon as Jake had assured her she'd be fine, she'd relaxed.

Ranger had been belligerent, arguing that he felt fine and complaining that Shash needed him in engineering.

He'd scowled and huffed as Jake had checked him over, but that kind of behavior was completely normal for him. If he'd been subdued or cooperative, that would have raised red flags. Instead, he'd passed the examination with flying colors.

Pine had cracked morbid jokes and shared grisly stories of the injuries he'd seen from other explosions he'd survived, pausing only when Isin asked him a question. He'd acted like he wasn't the least bit concerned about what Jake was doing until it came time to hear the final report. He'd fallen silent, his hands clenched in his lap, his gaze slightly over Jake's shoulder until he'd been given a clean bill of health.

Camp had sat quietly while Jake worked, not asking questions, and responding to Isin's queries with an easygoing manner that didn't fit his personality or the potential radiation scenario they'd created. The monotone of his replies had a pleasantly robotic quality, revealing how hard he was focusing on not tipping his hand.

Now came the challenging part—getting Camp to the brig. He was a big man. And powerful. He also kept weapons in his cabin. Taking him quietly wouldn't be easy.

But that wasn't what bothered Isin. He hadn't used the cells since taking over as captain. In truth, he'd avoided even thinking about that part of the ship. Shim had enjoyed keeping the cells filled, putting crew and captives together in combinations guaranteed to cause conflict. He'd considered it a bonus whenever the crew had to pull a corpse out of a cell following the night cycle.

"Problem, Captain?"

Isin glanced up.

Jake was watching him with the same analytical expression he had when puzzling over a medical problem.

"Just deciding the best way to get Camp to the brig."

"I wouldn't worry about that." Jake leaned against the med platform and folded his arms, the picture of nonchalance.

"Why not?"

"That injection I gave him? The one I said would counteract radiation toxicity? It was a sedative. He should be easy to manage in about five minutes."

"You sedated them all?" Jake had given all four crewmembers an injection before releasing them, waiting until the next person was in the room so they'd believe it was standard procedure. But Isin had assumed it was a ruse.

"No, just Camp. The other three received a placebo." Jake's gaze flicked to the closed door. "That explosion could have killed someone. Sedation seemed... appropriate."

The medic had just made Isin's job a hundred times easier. He clapped him on the shoulder. "Thanks."

"Anything to help." Jake nodded to one of the drawers. "And I have more of that sedative, if you need it."

Isin crossed to the door. "Let's hope I don't."

Twenty-One

Subduing Camp was a snap. Isin contacted Sweep, who met him in the corridor outside Camp's cabin. They found him slumped against his bunk, snoring.

Dragging his dead weight up the stairs and along the corridor to the brig was another matter. It was like dancing with an elephant. The workout had Isin dripping with sweat by the time Camp was stretched out on the sleeping platform with the cell door closed and locked.

Sweep propped his shoulders against the bulkhead and leaned his head back, his breath coming in and out in short bursts. "Next time, ask Jake to use a milder sedative."

"Good idea." Isin swiped the top of his head with the sleeve of his tunic. "I think Camp's been enjoying more than his fair share of beer."

"No kidding." Sweep pulled a square of cloth from his pocket and mopped the perspiration running down his face. "What's the next move?"

"I'll check in with Shash and Itorye on the engine repairs. What's the status on the shields and weapons?"

"The system's fine, but most of the power lines to the engine room were fried. I've been working on replacing them, but it would go faster if I had help."

"Do you trust Shorty and Summer?"

"Not as much as Fleur and Avril, but I have trouble picturing them aligning with Camp."

"Me, too. I'll release them both under your supervision. I'm also sending Willow, Ranger, and Pine to help Shash and Itorye. The rest of the crew can stay in lockdown for now."

"You think Camp isn't our only traitor?"

"I don't know, but I'm not taking any chances. We don't have time to question everyone."

When he returned to the engine room, he found Itorye in front of the main console, studying the diagnostic information scrolling across the surface. "Where's Shash?"

"Here." A hand waved at him from an open access panel near the deck. Shash appeared a moment later, wiping her hands on a towel. "What did you find out?"

"Camp."

Shash let loose with a string of curses and a look worthy of Medusa. "That double-crossing son of a bitch! I'll castrate him for this."

Itorye's response was quieter, but no less intense. "Gutting him would be more fitting."

The glance the two women shared made Isin very glad he wasn't in Camp's shoes. He hadn't decided how he'd deal with their saboteur, but he might allow Shash to make the final determination and carry out the sentence. After all, Camp had been working under her supervision. She deserved a say in his punishment. "I'm calling Willow, Ranger, and Pine in to help with repairs."

"Fine." Shash stalked back to the access panel, grumbling insults aimed at Camp under her breath.

Isin contacted the trio and told them to report to the engine room. Then he turned to Itorye. "How close are we to getting the engines operational?"

"Camp knew just where to hit us. We might be able to get enough power to the main engines to move the ship into orbit in about an hour."

"Good. I'll—"

Sweep's voice came over the comm. "We've got an incoming ship."

Isin shot a look at Itorye. "You don't have an hour."

Twenty-Two

Isin made it to the bridge in six seconds. "Talk to me."

"Armored freighter class warship in visual range." Sweep indicated the small object on the port bridgescreen. "We would have missed it if I hadn't stopped in to check the sensor readings." He looked pointedly at Byrd, who was slouched in the navigator's chair.

Isin bypassed the captain's platform, moving right beside Byrd. "Why didn't you see it? You were supposed to be watching for ships."

The pilot avoided his gaze. "I was watching."

"With your eyes closed?"

"No."

Isin pivoted Byrd's chair and leaned down so they were eye to eye. "When this is over, you and I are going to have a little chat."

Byrd looked away. "Yeah, sure."

The insolence in the pilot's voice triggered a flare of heat in Isin's blood. It took every bit of willpower he possessed to keep from hauling Byrd out of the chair and marching him to the Cage. Itorye could take over at the helm, but he'd need her at tactical as soon as the engines came online. And with Kenji on *Phoenix*, he didn't have a pilot to spare.

He unclenched his fingers from the back of Byrd's chair and turned to Sweep. "Estimated ETA?"

"Ten minutes at present speed."

The image on the bridgescreen behind Sweep showed a vessel with less than half the armor of *Vengeance*, and smaller by two-thirds. Ordinarily, *Vengeance* could take on a ship like that easily. But there was nothing ordinary about their current situation.

"What's their weapons complement?"

Sweep checked the readout. "Class A particle cannons and high-yield torpedoes. Powerful enough to penetrate the hull plating if they get through our shields."

"Status on our shields?"

"Operational, but we're still on auxiliary power and working with damaged lines. We have thirty percent fore and aft and forty percent port and starboard."

"And the weapons?"

"Same story. We only have enough juice for a few shots. Summer and Shorty are working on the damaged lines."

"How long until they're finished?"

Sweep shook his head. "Too long."

Not the answer he wanted. Until *Vengeance* could move, they'd be an easy target. He opened a channel to the engine room. "Itorye, give me good news."

"Good news? I've got bad news and worse news." Itorye sounded calm, but Shash's barked commands and the rattle and bang of metal on metal in the background painted a different picture. "We might have minimal engine power in five minutes."

"You've got four." He turned to Sweep. "Shields up as soon as they're in weapons range."

"Aye."

"Byrd, plot a course to the gas giant. The second those engines come online, punch it. Don't wait for a command." Most mercenaries thrived on violence, but a smart mercenary knew when *not* to fight. "If they—" He cut off as the external comm light flashed, indicating an incoming hail from the approaching vessel.

The captain of the other ship wanted to talk? Fine. He'd gladly have a chat if it bought his crew time for repairs. He moved to the captain's chair and set the bridge camera to zoom in on his face before putting the incoming feed on the bridgescreen. A close-up of his scar usually intimidated his adversaries.

Not this time. The captain of the other vessel had already seen it.

Kerr stared down at him, larger than life. "Hello, traitor."

Twenty-Three

Isin's fingers gripped the arms of his chair, but he kept his expression neutral. No point in giving Kerr the satisfaction of a reaction.

Kerr had set his bridge camera to give a wide-angle view, allowing Isin to see four of his lackeys at their stations, including Rossi, the pilot he'd recognized on Gallows Edge.

Kerr's lips tilted up in a mocking smile. "What? No greeting? I'm hurt."

Isin didn't voice the greeting that came to mind. "Why are you here?"

"Why? I'm here to help."

"We don't need your help."

Kerr made a *tsk-tsk* noise. "Oh, you misunderstand me. I'm not here to help *you*. I'm here to help myself. I'm reclaiming my ship and sending your worthless carcass into space."

Isin bared his teeth in a grim smile. "Try it."

"Oh, I'll do far more than try. As crippled as you are, you're no match for *Viper*. I made sure of it."

"By colluding with Camp." Too bad he couldn't have taken Camp to the Cage instead of the brig and worked him over. If Camp hadn't been sedated, he could have gotten Kerr's name out of the worthless dung heap. And he might have felt better, too.

"You figured that out? Very good." His patronizing tone scraped up Isin's spine. "I expected you to still be chasing your tail."

"Sorry to disappoint."

"Oh, you are a disappointment, in so many ways. But not for long."

"Meaning what?"

"Meaning I'm taking *Vengeance*." Kerr leaned forward, like he was about to impart a secret. "But if you surrender yourself to me, I promise the rest of your crew will not be harmed."

Sweep snorted. "You're a few cards short of a full deck if you think that will happen."

"I heard that." Kerr's gaze shifted slightly to his right, even though he wouldn't be able to see Sweep on the video feed. "Glad to know you're still onboard, Sweep. We have unfinished business as well." His eyes gleamed with malice.

"Yes, we do." Sweep sounded calm, but a thread of iron underlay his words. He had months of torment to repay.

Kerr's attention shifted back to Isin. "So what will it be? A dignified surrender and safety for your crew? Or a massacre?"

Isin used his peripheral vision to check the chronometer. He needed to buy Itorye and Shash another minute or two at least. "What makes you think you can defeat me? You know the power of this ship."

"Oh, Isin. Bluffing? Is that what we've come to? Or could it be you don't yet realize the direness of your circumstances?"

Since Kerr seemed to be warming to the drama, Isin played along. Anything to keep the egomaniac talking. "Why don't you explain it to me?"

"I could, but that would take away the fun, wouldn't it?"

"Fun?"

"Oh, yes. I'm going to enjoy this immensely."

The deck beneath his boots vibrated. The engines were powering up.

"I've considered your proposal, Kerr." Isin tapped his chin in a show of deep thought. "Gracious as it is, I must decline." The vibration increased. "I'm sure you understand."

"Then you'll—"

Whatever Kerr said next was lost as Isin cut the transmission. *Vengeance* lurched forward, throwing Isin against his chair as the stabilizers worked to overcome the unconventional launch from a dead stop. The image of Kerr's ship shifted toward the rear bridgescreen as Byrd took *Vengeance* in a tight arc, headed for the gas giant.

Isin rotated his chair to keep Kerr's ship in his view. "Shields?"

"Forty-five percent to aft," Sweep confirmed. "Kerr's powering weapons."

He opened a comm channel to the engine room. "Itorye, we need more power to the engines."

Shash replied instead. "And I need an engine that's not threatening to explode. We both can dream."

"Where's Itorye?"

"Here," Itorye answered as she hurried onto the bridge and slid behind the tactical console. "Pulling up specs on the planet." She glanced over her shoulder at him. "Entering that atmosphere won't be easy."

As usual, she'd anticipated his plan. "But the radiation should keep their sensors from tracking us."

"Agreed."

Isin left her to deal with the planet while he focused on the rear bridgescreen. The image of Kerr's ship kept pace with them.

"They're firing."

Two torpedoes shot out of the tubes on either side of Kerr's ship and raced toward *Vengeance.*

"Evasive maneuvers!"

The bridgescreen image tilted as Byrd brought *Vengeance*'s nose down. One of the torpedoes shot over the ship's topline, but the other impacted, sending a tremor through the deck.

"Aft shields at thirty-three percent."

"Return fire!"

The momentary glow from *Vengeance*'s torpedoes disappeared rapidly into the black, headed for Kerr's ship.

Cannon fire lanced out to meet them, decimating one of the torpedoes in a brief flare of light. The other struck the ship's shields and exploded. The cannon fire continued, now targeting *Vengeance*'s shields.

The ship shuddered. "Shields down to eighteen percent," Sweep called out. "Power to weapons is falling. I can give you one more torpedo and then we're done."

"Hold." He pivoted to face Itorye. "Time to the upper cloud layer?"

"Sixteen seconds. And we're going to need those shields when we hit it."

He opened a comm channel. "Shash, can you give me more power to shields?"

"Oh, sure." Her sarcasm came through clearly.

"Pull it from engines if you have to." They wouldn't be leaving the area anytime soon.

"I'll see what I can do."

The gas giant filled the forward bridgescreen as the deck began to shake.

Isin fastened his shoulder harness a moment before Byrd pitched *Vengeance* into a dive, the cannon fire from Kerr's ship creating a bizarre kaleidoscope effect in the clouds. A few seconds later the planet's upper gas layer engulfed the ship, the deck shoving against the bottom of Isin's boots as the combination of the planet's gravitational pull and the cloud turbulence tossed them like driftwood on a rough sea.

A flare of light brightened the starboard bridgescreen and the ship bucked.

"Torpedo hit the starboard shields," Sweep informed him. "Down to twenty-four percent."

Isin turned to Itorye. "Where's Kerr's ship?"

"Last sensor contact put him at thirty degrees to starboard."

Cannon fire illuminated the cloud layer, but nothing struck the shields.

"Did he follow us into the atmosphere?"

"Hard to tell, but I don't think so."

The ship continued to rattle and shake, but not from weapons fire. The bridgescreen visual was a wash of colors that jiggled and danced as the imaging system struggled to compensate for the intense vibrations caused by the planet's atmosphere.

"Byrd, move us off." Isin gripped the armrests as the deck lurched. "Try to find calm air."

"What do you think I'm doing?" Byrd muttered, his focus on his console.

Isin let the comment slide. Now wasn't the time for a showdown.

The clouds glowed in alternating flares of orange, yellow, and red, but fainter than before. Kerr was either far behind them, or keeping his ship out of the planet's atmosphere.

Predictable. The man was a coward at heart. He wouldn't chase prey when he thought he might lose. Out there, he was in control. In here, the planet took charge.

The shaking subsided, the clouds dissipating to offer a vista that stretched a few kilometers into the distance.

"Found calm air." Byrd delivered the information with a slight smirk.

"Keep it that way." Isin pivoted to Sweep. "Shield status?"

"Holding. No radiation leaks yet, but without more power, that won't last."

"Weapons?"

"Not until we repair those electrical lines."

Isin glanced at the bridgescreen. The flashes in the clouds had almost stopped, but given time, Kerr might change his mind about coming in after them. Patience wasn't one of his virtues. "Itorye can monitor the situation here. Go help Shorty and Summer with the repairs. I want full weapons and shields in an hour."

Sweep didn't question the timetable, but the set of his jaw as he left the bridge didn't inspire hope.

Isin opened a channel. "Shash, what's your status?"

"That hard launch blew one of the patches. It's a mess down here." And she sounded royally ticked off about it.

"Do you need more hands?" Six members of the crew were still locked in their quarters, no doubt wondering what the hell was going on. Unless of course they were working with Kerr and Camp, in which case they knew exactly what was going on. He'd have to address that problem eventually, but it could wait.

"No. I've already got the three that are worth anything. Or are you volunteering? I can certainly put your muscles to work."

He ignored the none-too-subtle come on. That kind of talk was as natural to Shash as breathing. He'd gladly do anything to prevent the planet's radiation from eating away at the ship's shields and hull. And killing the crew.

He turned to Itorye. "I'll be in engineering."

Twenty-Four

"If we stay in the planet's atmosphere another hour, the crew will die from radiation exposure."

Isin looked up from the main engine room console and met Jake's gaze. "But we're still an hour away from getting the shields and weapons to full strength."

Jake's brown eyes reflected his inner calm... and determination. "There's only so much I can do to counteract the effects. The shields weren't designed to repel this level of radiation. It's leaking into the ship. We have to leave."

Isin returned his attention to the diagnostic data. "We've only restored fifty-three percent power to the weapons, and sixty-four percent power to shields. Interstellar engines are dead in the water. If we leave the planet's atmosphere, we have nowhere to go. Kerr knows this ship. He'll hit us where it counts." Or worse, Kerr could have another nasty surprise up his sleeve.

"I understand the problem. But this pocket of cloudless air we're in is acting like a greenhouse on the radiation, concentrating the levels to twice that of the surrounding clouds. At the very least you need to take us into the upper cloud layer. Anything to decrease the radiation levels."

Isin shook his head. "The upper layer will shake the ship like a toy in a dog's mouth. We can't work on the engine repairs under those conditions."

"If you don't move the ship pretty soon, you won't be doing *any* repairs because the crew won't be able to stand."

     Audrey Sharpe

Isin gripped the edge of the console. *Damned if I do, damned if I don't.*

"Isin? You know I'm right."

"Yeah, I do. I just don't like it." He blew out a breath. He wasn't arguing with Jake because he disagreed. It was just a way to vent some of his frustration. "What's the current exposure level?"

"Sixty-five percent of lethal tolerance in the outer decks, forty-eight percent on the bridge. The drugs and equipment I have onboard can treat the effects up to seventy-five percent. If exposure goes beyond that, the cellular damage will be permanent."

"What's our max time allotment?"

The corners of Jake's mouth tightened. "I can give you eighteen minutes. After that, you're rolling the dice." He strode out of the engine room as Isin returned his focus to the console.

Eighteen minutes. The ship wouldn't be anywhere close to fully functional by then. Camp had done a masterful job. Shash had informed him that they didn't even have the replacement part they needed for the interstellar engines onboard.

That wasn't an accident. According to her inventory, the storage locker that should have held the unit was mysteriously empty. Camp must have made it disappear in the reclamation center. Or he could have hidden it somewhere on the ship, ready to be handed over to Kerr after they'd pulled off their sabotage and ambush plan.

Shash had agreed to work on an alternative, but she'd said it like she knew it was what he needed to hear, not because she believed she could do it. And if Shash couldn't do it, no one could.

Which left him to face Kerr with a cobbled together main engine and partially functional weapons and shields, or remain in the planet's atmosphere and accept certain death.

An awful choice, but fairly easy to make. He'd rather take his chances with Kerr than slowly poison his crew. Most mercenaries expected to die fighting, anyway.

He walked into the compartment where Shash and Ranger were working on the repairs. "You have ten minutes to finish what you're doing. Then we're leaving this planet."

Shash scowled. "But the engines aren't—"

"We're slowly cooking in the planet's radiation field. Ten minutes. That's it."

Her jaw clenched. "Fine."

He headed for the bridge. If they got lucky, they'd exit the planet's atmosphere without being detected by Kerr. The gas giant's sheer size might conceal them long enough that they could finish repairs to the shields and weapons. That wouldn't solve the interstellar drive issue, but they didn't need it to defeat Kerr.

Byrd and Itorye were gathered at the navigation console when Isin walked onto the bridge.

Itorye straightened. "How are the repairs coming?"

"The radiation levels are rising too quickly to continue. We have to leave."

She nodded, like she'd been expecting the announcement. "Will a high orbit put us out of danger?"

"From the radiation? Probably."

"But not Kerr."

"No."

"Which is why we have an alternative. The planet's fifth moon should be in orbit above us."

"You've been able to chart our relative position?"

"As best I can, given the limited data."

"And that helps us how?"

"We might be able to use the moon as a home base to finish repairs. The stellar database indicates the moon has a thin atmosphere and a density consistent with a rocky core. If we can reach it without being detected, we could land on the surface and go to minimal power while we work on repairs."

Their odds had just improved. "Distance to the moon?"

"Six hundred twenty thousand kilometers."

Not exactly around the block. It was a gamble, either way. But they couldn't use the planet's atmosphere as cover anymore, not without risking lethal exposure to the radiation.

The moon could provide temporary sanctuary—if they reached it safely. A big if, but better than sitting out in the open, waiting for Kerr to circle the planet and spot them.

"Lay in the flight plan." Isin dropped into the captain's chair and opened a comm channel. "Sweep, I need you on the bridge."

"On my way."

"Speaking of Kerr, have you seen any more weapons fire from his ship?"

"Not in the last hour."

"Then let's hope he's sitting on the opposite side of the planet." He switched the comm to the engine room. "Shash, is everything secure?"

"For now."

"Keep me informed if anything changes."

"I always do," she grumbled.

Sweep strode onto the bridge and settled at his station as Isin closed the channel.

"Weapons status?"

Sweep pivoted to face him. "The lines to the cannons are solid. The torpedoes are touch and go. I might be able to give you twenty, or two."

But the cannons were more powerful at close range. If Kerr wanted to board *Vengeance*, he'd have to get *really* close. "Don't wait for my signal. Fire at any target you see."

The lines around Sweep's eyes and mouth deepened. "Aye."

Isin shifted his attention to Byrd. "Bring us out as slowly as you can without shaking the ship apart. Itorye, scan for Kerr's ship."

Itorye moved to tactical and strapped in while Byrd followed Isin's command.

The image on the bridgescreen shifted, the upper cloud layer descending as the ship rose to meet it. The deck began to shake as they entered the turbulent outer layer of the gas giant's atmosphere. Isin gripped the arm rests, his harness pressing against his shoulders and chest as the swirling orange, pink, and tan clouds enveloped them, rushing past the ship's cameras. The deck bucked, the vibrations from the engines growing stronger as the ship fought to escape the turbulence and the planet's gravity. The clouds thinned, the faint glimmer of stars appearing through the gaps.

The ship's motion smoothed out.

"Any sign of Kerr?"

Itorye shook her head without looking up from her console. "Not yet."

One piece of good news. They continued to climb, the clouds parting and the stars gaining strength as the main engines thrust the ship forward like a cannonball. The gas giant's fifth moon glowed in the distance, a faint half circle that grew steadily larger.

"Byrd, get us to that moon. Best possible speed."

"On it."

Isin rotated his chair, watching the aft camera view of the enormous planet. He'd never be able to see Kerr's ship on the bridgescreen before Itorye picked it up on sensors, but illogical as it might be, he didn't like having his back to his adversary.

"Distance to the moon?" he called out after several minutes passed in silence.

"Three hundred thousand kilometers."

Halfway there. The image of the planet hadn't changed appreciably, although it wasn't filling as much space on the right and left sides of the bridgescreen.

Isin glanced over his shoulder at Byrd. "When we reach the moon, take us to the dark side and scan—"

"I've spotted Kerr's ship," Itorye cut in. "He's coming around the planet to starboard."

A string of curses spilled from Isin's lips. "Has he seen us?"

"Yes. He's adjusting course and accelerating to intercept."

"Can we get to the moon before he reaches us?"

Itorye's lips compressed. "It'll be close."

Isin opened a comm channel. "Shash, we need more power to the engines."

"Are you nuts? We just patched this thing back together and you want to tear it apart?"

"If Kerr catches us, you won't be worrying about damaged engines." Shash had been a member of the crew under Shim and Kerr's reign. He doubted she was eager for a reunion.

Her reply confirmed it. "I'll see what I can do."

Isin kept his gaze on the approaching ship, visible as a dark spot against the vibrant colors of the gas giant. "Distance to the moon?"

"One hundred thirty kilometers."

But the dark spot kept getting larger. *Vengeance* was a great ship, but even at her best, she was built for power and durability, not speed. He glanced at the moon. Still too far away.

His gaze met Itorye's. The same understanding showed in her dark eyes.

They weren't going to win this foot race.

Twenty-Five

The first torpedoes struck *Vengeance* thirty-five thousand kilometers from the moon.

"Aft shields at forty-one percent." Lights flared on the bridgescreen as Sweep sent an answering torpedo back at Kerr's ship.

"Bring us around!" Isin barked at Byrd. "Get us nose-to-nose with that monster."

"But, Capt—"

"Do it!"

Byrd paled, but followed the order. The bridgescreen image shifted, the moon sliding to starboard, bringing Kerr's ship front and center.

Sweep unleashed a series of torpedoes now that the ship's forward facing arsenal was available, but only one struck Kerr's ship. The torpedoes from Kerr's ship lit up *Vengeance*'s shields, the deck quaking under Isin's boots.

"Forward shields at thirty-two percent."

"Damage to their ship?"

"Minimal. Our torpedo targeting is slightly misaligned. I'm compensating."

Kerr's ship banked, showing the dorsal side.

"He's flanking!" Isin warned. "Keep us—"A jolt knocked him sideways in his chair.

"Torpedoes are offline!" Sweep barked.

"Byrd! I told you to keep us facing him!"

"I'm trying."

"Don't try. *Do it!*"

Another jolt shook the ship.

"We've lost portside thrusters, too," Itorye informed him, much more calmly than the situation warranted.

"I'm losing maneuverability," Byrd confirmed.

"Cannons?"

Sweep shook his head. "Out of range."

And they were out of options. If he didn't act soon, Kerr's ship would pummel them with torpedoes without ever presenting a target. "Ramming speed. Full ahead."

Byrd's jaw sagged open. "But—"

"*Now!*" Isin's roar echoed off the bulkheads. He opened a shipwide channel as Byrd snapped back to face his console. "All crew, brace for impact."

Vengeance's prow had been designed as a vertical battering ram. A strong enough collision could cripple or destroy an enemy ship. Isin had been onboard the last time it had been used. Their opponent's vessel had broken in two.

The deck vibration increased as the ship surged forward.

Isin gripped the arms of his chair, his focus on their target.

And then the navigation console exploded, flinging Byrd to the floor in a shower of sparks.

Twenty-Six

Isin was out of his chair and crouched beside Byrd in seconds.

The pilot lay crumpled on his side, his cheek pressed to the deck and scorch marks on his skin and clothing. But he was still breathing.

"Get Jake up here," Isin shouted amidst the chaotic bangs and rattles as Kerr's ship resumed the attack.

As Itorye followed his order, he dropped into the navigator's chair and swiped his forearm across the console to dislodge the debris. Not that it mattered. Whatever electrical charge had blasted through had obliterated the controls. The hunk of charred metal wasn't good for anything but scrap.

Abandoning the station, he staggered like a drunken sailor as another jolt struck the ship. He fought to maintain his balance as he climbed the steps to the captain's chair. "Itorye, reroute navigation to your console. Engines fu–"

A series of concussive booms drowned out his command and the deck trembled like the ship was caught in an earthquake. He made a lunge for the chair, latching on with one hand, his muscles straining as he struggled to keep his grip.

"Shields are down!" Sweep yelled over the blasts that rocked the ship. "We just lost our lateral weapons array."

Isin's gaze snapped to the bridgescreen. Kerr had taken full advantage of their momentary incapacitation, moving his ship out of *Vengeance's* path and coming alongside.

So much for ramming him. Or disabling him with the cannons.

A blur of movement on the bridgescreen was followed by dull thumps that resounded through the ship's hull.

"Grapplers," Sweep confirmed.

"Itorye, can you pull us free?"

"I can't do anything. Navigation commands aren't responding."

Isin smacked the comm. "Shash, I need power to the engines!"

"They're fried," Shash barked back. "A surge came through here that blew half the connections. *Vengeance* isn't going anywhere."

No shields. No weapons. No engines. What next?

Isin turned at the sound of footsteps. Jake appeared through the back hatch, med kit in hand, looking like he'd gone ten rounds with a grizzly. "Stairs were fun," he murmured as he hurried to where Byrd lay on the deck.

Squeals of metal on metal reverberated through the hull as the image of Kerr's ship drew steadily closer.

"They're reeling us in," Sweep said.

"Can you get the lateral cannons online?"

Sweep shook his head. "Even if they were functional, we can't fire them at this distance. We'd do more damage to *Vengeance* than Kerr's ship."

"Then we'd better prepare for a boarding party." They may have lost the battle, but there was no way he would lose the war. "Shash, seal off the engine room. We're about to have company."

"Wonderful. I needed something to do."

He ignored the sarcasm. "Just don't do anything reckless." Chaos tended to follow in her wake.

"Me? Never."

He bit his tongue. He didn't have time to lecture her. She was going to do what she was going to do. He closed the channel and turned to Sweep. "Seal the blast doors on all exterior docking ports, then have the crew report to the armory."

"All the crew?"

He still had six crewmembers on lockdown who could be friend or foe. But he needed all the help they could get. "Yes. I'll meet you in the armory in two minutes."

Twenty-Seven

Vengeance groaned and shuddered as Isin made his way to his cabin. It would take Kerr at least ten minutes to align the ships for docking. The blast doors might buy them another ten or fifteen, although Kerr was resourceful enough to have planned for that eventuality. He might have a trick or two up his sleeve.

Isin had a new appreciation for how Sisyphus had felt pushing that boulder up a hill only to have it roll back down. Inside his cabin, he quickly donned his armor and snagged weapons and ammunition from his personal arsenal. His gaze passed over the panel concealing the cube. Delivering it to Green had become the least of his concerns.

With *Vengeance's* engines and weapons down, the only way to win was by taking control of Kerr's ship. Unfortunately, he was going in blind, while Kerr knew *Vengeance* as well as he did. All the cards were stacked in Kerr's favor.

Which was exactly how Kerr had planned it. Coward.

He met up with Willow and Ranger in the corridor. They were dressed in the battle gear favored by most of the members of his crew. The black mesh material clung to their bodies like a second skin but had a tensile strength that could deflect a knife point. They also wore armor plating similar to Isin's, and holsters that provided ample locations to tuck weapons.

"Captain." Ranger nodded at him, his dark eyes gleaming with the light of battle. One thing about mercenaries—they were always up for a fight.

Shorty and Summer were already in the armory, working with Sweep to dispense weapons to the crew. The six who'd been on lockdown looked a little disgruntled, but compared to life with Shim and Kerr, the past day had been a picnic. Needles and Downey made muttered comments about Kerr's questionable parentage, which underscored that fact.

Tremors continued to ripple up through the deck. A quick check of the security monitor confirmed Kerr's ship was aligning with the portside airlock on C deck.

Isin moved next to Sweep, keeping his voice low so the crew wouldn't overhear. "Any brilliant ideas?"

Sweep glanced at the monitor, the tendons in his neck flexing. "He knows this ship as well as we do."

"But he doesn't know *us* half as well as he thinks he does."

Sweep's dark eyes lit with understanding. "You want to play off his overconfidence?"

"It's his greatest weakness."

"And easy to manipulate." Sweep studied the image of Kerr's ship. "He already knows *Vengeance* is dead in the water. He'll be coming after you."

"And he'll expect me to be on the bridge."

"That's right."

"So I won't be." The best way to stay one step ahead of him was to be unpredictable. He motioned to the monitor. "What can you tell me about his ship?"

"It's a standard freighter class Nova 4 modified for assault."

"Are you familiar with the ship's layout?"

"Yep. Been on several Novas. They've upgraded a few things in the Nova 4, but the layout's pretty much the same."

"How hard would it be to crack the ship's security system?"

"Depends on what you're trying to accomplish. And where you gain access. What do you have in mind?"

"While our crew leads Kerr on a wild goose chase through *Vengeance,* I want to take over his ship."

"How?"

Isin pointed to an exterior hatch on Kerr's ship one deck up from the airlock. "For starters, you're going to get me through that hatch."

Twenty-Eight

While Sweep went to the shuttle bay to fetch their spacesuits, Isin contacted Itorye. "Are Jake and Byrd still with you?"

"No. Byrd revived enough to make it to the infirmary."

"What's his condition?"

"He got scorched, but he'll be fine."

"Good. Seal off the bridge and join me in the armory."

"On my way."

He contacted Jake next. "Take whatever supplies you need and move Byrd to the *Dagger.*"

Jake sounded irritable. "He's in no condition to fly a transport."

"He won't be flying anywhere. But we're about to be boarded. You're a lot safer in the shuttle bay than the infirmary." The bay had four layers of interior shielding that isolated it from the rest of the ship. The design was intended to protect the ship in case the outer doors were damaged or a transport crashed during a landing. But it also made the bay a virtually impenetrable fortress against anyone trying to break in from the corridor.

The slight pause indicated Jake was pondering the scenario Isin had sketched out and reaching the same conclusion. "Give me five minutes."

"You have three. I'm sending Summer to help you."

Summer nodded, slinging her rifle over her shoulder and exiting the armory, passing Itorye coming in.

Isin met Itorye halfway. "Sweep and I are taking a space walk to Kerr's ship. You're in charge of keeping his boarding party busy playing hide and seek."

A gleam of anticipation lit Itorye's dark eyes. "That'll be fun."

"I assigned Summer to guard Jake and Byrd in the shuttle bay. The rest of the crew is at your disposal."

"What about Camp? Kerr may try to free him."

Isin's jaw clenched. He'd forgotten about the traitor locked in the brig. "Ask Jake how soon the sedative will wear off. If Camp's drugged, he's not a threat. If he's awake—" Isin held her gaze. "Neutralize him. Your discretion."

He left Itorye to marshal the crew while he met up with Sweep outside the shuttle bay. Voices from the stairwell drew his attention as Jake, Byrd, and Summer made their way down to the bay. Jake and Summer were supporting the pilot, his arms over their shoulders.

"Almost there." Jake's tone conveyed the perfect combination of empathy and encouragement guaranteed to keep his patient moving.

Byrd seemed disoriented, stumbling and leaning heavily on Summer. She listed toward the bulkhead as his feet threatened to tangle with hers. She shot Jake a look and he pulled Byrd's lanky form upright, adjusting the bulky medical pack slung across his chest.

Isin moved to intercept them as they reached the deck. "Do you have everything you need?"

Jake's brows lifted a fraction. "For now." His gaze swept over the spacesuit in Isin's hands. "But not if I'll be treating major injuries."

"Not planning on any major injuries."

"You never do."

The clanks of a spacebridge connecting with the airlock drifted down from C deck.

Isin indicated the shuttle bay with a lift of his chin. "Get inside. We'll seal the doors so you shouldn't have any unexpected visitors." His gaze moved to Summer. "No one comes through this door expect me, Sweep, or Itroye."

She fingered the pistol strapped to her hip. "No problem."

The trio hobbled to the *Dagger* as the bay doors slid closed. Isin engaged the additional security, a thicker door dropping down from above to seal off access to the main door and the control panel, while two more doors closed in the bay's interior. Isin keyed in the code to put the bay in full security mode and turned to Sweep. "Let's go."

Twenty-Nine

The shuddering had ceased by the time Isin and Sweep reached the exterior maintenance hatch on A deck. A quick check of the monitor in the antechamber confirmed Kerr's ship was snugged up to *Vengeance*, a short spacebridge extending between them like a mosquito's proboscis puncturing skin.

Isin set down his rifle and made quick work of pulling on his spacesuit. Securing the helmet in place, he switched on the display for his faceplate, checking the feed from the bubble camera attached to the outside of the hatch. It gave him a view of both ships and the line of grappler cables holding them together. The sight made his blood run hot, but he shoved his emotions aside. He'd need a cool head to pull this off.

He scanned the image until he spotted their target—the exterior hatch on Kerr's ship.

Sweep's voice came over the suit's comm. "Ready when you are." He'd already donned one of the propulsion packs secured in storage racks attached to the bulkhead.

Isin slipped the shoulder straps of another one over the padded fabric of his suit and secured the pack in place. "Let's go."

Sweep closed the interior hatch for the anteroom, sealing them inside and depressurizing the tiny space.

Isin climbed the short ladder to the exterior hatch and keyed in the command to unlock it. As the hatch swung open, the starfield spread out before him, drawing him out of the confines of the ship. He magnetized his boots and stepped onto the hull, the connection forming a solid bond.

Sweep followed, closing the hatch behind them.

Isin crouched next to the nearest grappler line. The narrow stretch of cable would be relatively easy to cut through with the right tools, but there was no point. With the engines down, disengaging from Kerr's ship would make *Vengeance* more vulnerable, not less. If he wanted to get out of this, he had to go to the source of his problems. Kerr.

The hatch they wanted was four meters forward and two meters below their current location. And what do you know? One of the grappler cables was right next to it. They could use the cable as a conduit rather than the propulsion packs.

Attaching their towlines to the cable and walking hand over hand to their destination took less than a minute. Overriding the hatch's security and safety protocols without triggering an alarm wasn't quite so simple, but the security system hadn't been invented that Sweep couldn't crack.

Isin stood guard while Sweep worked. They'd had no indication anyone on Kerr's ship was aware of their presence, but he wasn't taking any chances. He didn't want to lose the element of surprise.

"Got it."

Isin stepped into position, holding his rifle like a club as Sweep pulled open the hatch. The weapon wouldn't fire in the vacuum of space, but it would work as a blunt instrument if anyone was waiting for them on the other side.

The antechamber was empty.

Isin eased inside first, keeping one hand on the rifle and one on the ladder rungs. Sweep followed him down. The room was even smaller than the one on *Vengeance*, making it easy to check the porthole in the interior hatch. The corridor outside looked vacant. With any luck, Kerr had sent most of his crew to *Vengeance*, leaving his own ship virtually unprotected. Arrogance overriding common sense.

Sweep sealed the outer hatch and started the cycle to pressurize the compact space.

When the display flashed green, Isin opened the interior hatch, rifle at the ready. Sweep moved beside him as they stepped into the corridor, panning their weapons left and right. Nothing. For the moment they were alone.

Returning to the antechamber, Isin removed his helmet. The air on this ship tasted stale, like it had been recirculated through filters well past their expiration date. Probably true. Kerr never had been one for routine maintenance.

Sweep was already halfway out of his suit, so Isin quickly stripped off his, tucking it alongside Sweep's in a corner of the antechamber.

Adjusting his armor and strapping on his weapons, he glanced at Sweep. "Where to?"

"Engine room. Follow me."

Thirty

Sweep led the way along two short corridors lined with storage lockers and down a steep stairway. He halted at a T-junction at the bottom, lifting a hand.

Isin listened, picking up the murmur of voices.

"Two in the engine room," Sweep confirmed under his breath.

"How do you want to play this?"

In answer, Sweep pulled a circular disk from a side pocket of his vest. Crouching, he slid the object along the deck and into the engine room like a hockey puck into a goal.

The conversation ceased, replaced with violent coughing and the thump of unsteady footfalls, followed by two loud thuds.

"The gas won't dissipate for five minutes." Sweep removed two small ventilators from the same pocket and handed one to Isin. "You'll need this."

Isin attached the device over his nose and mouth, securing the band around his head as Sweep did the same. Sweep's resourcefulness continued to amaze him. The man seemed to have a solution for every potential encounter.

They slipped into the engine room. Sweep moved to the console bookended by Kerr's unconscious crewmembers. He tapped on the screen, then grunted. "Primary systems access is restricted to the bridge."

"Figures. Kerr wouldn't trust his own crew. Can you override?"

"Give me a moment."

Isin secured the room while Sweep worked, closing and sealing a second hatch at the opposite end, although he couldn't set a lock.

By the time he returned to the primary console, Sweep had brought up a pattern of square tiles depicting video feeds from *Vengeance.* The images moved, indicating Kerr's forces were using helmet cams. Not surprising. The cameras would allow Kerr to keep track of the fight without leaving the safety of the bridge. He always preferred to have his minions do the dirty work. It would also allow him to coordinate the assault.

Most of the images revealed darkened, empty rooms and corridors, but the tile showing *Vengeance*'s mess hall flashed with weapons fire. Figures moved in the background, the image jostling as Kerr's people pursued Isin's crew.

He glanced at Sweep. "Can you cut the feed from those cameras?"

"Working on it."

Isin opened a channel. "Itorye?"

Her voice came over the line in a hushed whisper. "A little busy right now."

"Kerr's using helmet cams to track you."

"How many?"

"Five—two on C deck, two on B deck, one on A deck. Sweep's working to cut the feed."

"Where exactly on B deck?"

"Port corridor outside engineering, and crew corridor just past Summer's cabin."

Isin's gaze darted to the screen as the whine of weapons fire screeched in his ear. The camera feed in the crew corridor lit up like a supernova, then went dark.

Itorye's voice replaced the cacophony, smooth as glass. "Any other tips?"

A grim smile tugged at his mouth. "C deck group is in the Mess and the A deck group's moving to the forward stairwell." If they converged, it would put Itorye's contingent between them.

"Got it."

More flashes on the monitor from the C deck camera were joined by the report of distant weapons fire over the comm. A silhouette fell across the image, landing on the floor in a heap. The camera moved in, light playing across Downey's face, his lips peeled back in a snarl as he struggled to lift his rifle with an arm charred to the bone. Another flash and Downey tumbled onto his back, his eyes glazing over.

Isin's fist curled and he pounded the console. "Sweep!"

"I know. Almost there."

Isin counted the seconds. One one thousand, two one thousand, three...

"Done." The monitor went blank. Sweep shot him a look. "Kerr will be able to trace the command to this console."

The whisper of hushed footsteps in the corridor drew Isin's attention to the hatch. "I think he already has."

Thirty-One

Isin shifted position, lining up a clear shot at the open hatch while Sweep moved to cover the closed back hatch.

Isin pressed against the bulkhead. They were likely to be outnumbered, but that was just fine. He was in a killing mood. And the gas hadn't finished dissipating, so that would slow down Kerr's crew.

The sounds in the corridor ceased, but a projectile sailed through the hatch and landed with a clatter on the deck. A cloud of smoky gas erupted from the cylinder, quickly filling the compartment. Apparently Sweep wasn't the only one who'd come prepared.

The ventilator Sweep had given him seemed to be keeping whatever reaction the gas was designed to cause at bay except a slight irritation to his eyes. But Kerr's crew didn't know that. When the first dark shape came through the hatch, Isin sent the man crashing to the ground in a lifeless heap with a single shot. The next two took critical wounds before clueing in that their prey wasn't incapacitated.

The hiss of the back hatch opening was followed by more shots, this time from Sweep's rifle, followed by the thump-thump of bodies striking the deck.

Blasts struck the bulkhead a meter from Isin's hiding place as two forms leaned in briefly through the hatch and fired before pulling back. Isin waited. The sequence was repeated, two more quick shots, both well wide of the mark and in an area where only an idiot would stand during a firefight. They weren't trying to hit him. They were just trying to distract him.

He darted a glance over his shoulder. Sweep was tough to see in the swirling mist, but he seemed to be in a similar situation, crouched behind a low console while blasts from the back hatch struck the bulkhead to his right.

Two more canisters sailed through the hatch, spraying white clouds of gas that completely obscured Isin's view of the entrance. He backed up and flattened his torso against the bulkhead, searching for movement in the swirling haze. No use. He couldn't see twenty centimeters in front of his face.

But neither could Kerr's people. Isin's eyes burned like kindling, so he closed them and listened. *There.* A faint footfall to his right, and another from behind, although he couldn't triangulate either. The gas seemed to be distorting sound, too.

Firing his rifle in these conditions would only help Kerr's people locate him. He needed stealth. Slipping his rifle over his shoulder, he exchanged it for the hunting knife strapped to his thigh.

A low hiss to his right, followed by another to his left, indicated Kerr's people had sealed both hatches, turning the engine room into a cage.

Isin's blood heated as his lips stretched in a feral smile. He had a lot of experience fighting in a cage.

Opening his eyes to slits, he searched for light changes in the shifting fog. When the first dark figure took form out of the mist, Isin struck, severing his enemy's carotid artery with a stroke of the blade. The clatter that followed as the body hit the floor disguised Isin's retreat. He pushed back in the direction he'd last seen Sweep. If they could coordinate—

He halted when two burly figures appeared in front of him, blocking his path.

He lunged at the closer of the two, but the man deflected the thrust of the blade with a mesh gauntlet, following up with a swing of a thick baton that grazed Isin's chin.

Isin couldn't return the favor thanks to the metal and spaceglass mask covering the man's face and neck, protecting him from the gas, and the cut of Isin's blade.

His companion wore one too, and also wielded a baton.

Moisture pooled on Isin's lower lashes, obscuring his vision as the gas gnawed at his corneas. He barely caught the movement as the second man swung the baton with surprising speed, aiming for Isin's torso.

Isin dodged, dropping low and slicing at his opponent's heel with his blade.

The muffled shriek that followed announced he'd succeeded in cutting the man's Achilles tendon.

Isin rolled to avoid the man's flailing form, crouching near the bulkhead. But his first opponent was waiting for him, baton already in motion. Isin pivoted, the club striking his shoulder blade, sending a shockwave of pain radiating over his back. He ignored it, continuing his movement and slashing at the man's leg.

But this one had learned from his friend's mistake. He sidestepped the stroke and kicked out, connecting with Isin's wrist and loosening his grip.

The blade sailed into the fog, striking a metallic surface with a dull clang.

Isin surged to his feet, catching his opponent off guard with a flying tackle that sent them both crashing to the ground. Taking advantage of his position, he wrapped his arm around the man's head. The mask might protect his opponent's face, but it wouldn't prevent Isin from snapping his neck.

The man bucked, trying to shake Isin off, but they were of similar height and weight, and Isin had leverage. He secured his grip as the man's hands scrambled to pry him off. Too late. One quick movement and the man lay lifeless in his arms.

And that's when the attack came. A blunt object struck the side of his head with enough force that he saw stars. He fell onto his side and sucked in air. Bad idea. The blow had dislodged his ventilator. Gas poured into his lungs.

The stars winked out. The last thing he saw before darkness closed in was the blurred outline of the man he'd hobbled stretched out on the deck with a baton lifted for a second swing.

Thirty-Two

"You continue to disappoint me."

Isin's head pounded like a drum and his mouth was dry as the Sahara, but he fought to pry his eyes open. He knew that voice.

He tried to lift his hand to his face, but his right arm screamed in protest while his left met with resistance. And an odd numbness.

"Go ahead and struggle," the voice continued. "It's highly entertaining."

He went still, giving his vision time to clear. The room slowly came into focus. He was in an infirmary, but the med platform pressed to his back had been inclined forty-five degrees, allowing him to look his enemy in the eyes without lifting his head.

Kerr stood two meters in front of him, gazing at him with his trademark smirk. "Really, Isin. I expected more of a fight from you."

Isin glanced down. His armor, weapons, and most of his clothes had been removed and tossed in a heap on the floor, leaving only his briefs. A pair of slim cylindrical metal restraints circled his arms above and below the elbow, with similar bands anchoring his legs above and below the knee, immobilizing him. No surprise there. Kerr would never dare face him in any other scenario.

Judging from the throbbing and swelling of his right wrist, the kick that had knocked away his knife had done some damage. But that wasn't what caused a tremor of alarm. He couldn't feel his left hand at all. It lay limp and lifeless against the white sheet covering the platform, with two small projections sticking out from the tips of his index and middle fingers. *The ends of hypodermic needles.* Which meant the needles themselves were inserted into his fingers.

What the hell was Kerr doing to him? He fixed his adversary with a look that could freeze the sun. "You want a fight? Undo these restraints and we'll fight." Even without the use of his hands, he could still take down a coward like Kerr.

"Oh, you'd like that wouldn't you? You were always eager to jump into the Cage." The corners of Kerr's mouth turned up in a mocking smile. "But I don't need to fight you. I've already won."

"Is that a fact?" Isin used his peripheral vision to scope out the room. He and Kerr were alone. No sign of Sweep, or anyone else. Had Sweep gotten away? Or was he locked up somewhere else?

Kerr gazed significantly at the restraints. "I would think the answer was obvious." The smirk grew into a chilling smile as his gaze moved to the needles. "Then again, I never credited you with much intelligence."

No, he hadn't. Which had played a big role in the success of Isin's coup on *Vengeance.* Kerr and Shim had always viewed him as a mindless brute, a belief he'd encouraged. Being underestimated was a powerful advantage.

But Kerr had managed to turn the tables. The assault in the engine room had been coordinated. Somehow, Kerr had figured out he was onboard.

Isin gave the needles a sidelong glance. And now he was paying the price.

"Curious?" Kerr crossed his arms over his chest and lounged against the bulkhead. "Tell me, can you feel anything below your wrist?"

Isin didn't bother to respond.

"I'll take that as a no. Don't worry. You will, soon enough."

The ominous words filled the room like a funeral dirge.

"Until then, we can have a little chat."

"Why don't you go take a space walk without a suit?"

"Really, Isin." Kerr shook his head like a disapproving parent. "You should be thanking me."

"Why's that?"

"Because I'm going to end your miserable existence."

The cruel gleam in Kerr's blue eyes made the acid in Isin's stomach churn. If he didn't figure a way off this table, Kerr might take him off it in pieces. Maybe the hypodermics were filled with poisons. Or corrosives.

He had to keep Kerr distracted while he formulated a plan. "What makes you think I'm miserable?"

Kerr made a flicking motion with his fingers, dismissing the question. "Again, obvious. Just look at you." His gaze wandered over the multitude of scars crisscrossing Isin's skin, his nose wrinkling in distaste. "I'll also be relieving you of the burden of your crew. Especially that sanctimonious bitch, Itorye."

A growl rumbled out of Isin's chest.

Kerr looked down his nose. "Ah, yes. You do have a thing for that whore, don't you?" His gaze shifted to the scar on Isin's cheek, his lip curling with disgust. "She deserves an ugly mongrel like you."

The bitterness in his words told the true story. Kerr had always coveted Itorye, but she'd rejected his advances. And since he had an ego the size of Jupiter, unrequited lust had turned into rage. The misogynistic prick hadn't even tweaked to the fact that Itorye preferred the company of women.

Kerr stepped closer, bringing his face level with Isin's. "Don't worry. You'll be seeing her again. In fact, I'm going to let you watch her die before I kill you."

Isin's fingers itched for his rifle—at least, the ones he could feel. Not that he could even grip a weapon if he had one. Lacking that, he mentally drilled a hole between Kerr's eyes.

Kerr, unfortunately, didn't drop dead. He planted his palms on Isin's chest and leaned in close enough that his vile breath wafted over Isin's mouth. "I have all *kinds* of ways to repay her. And I will. Over, and over, and over. It will be quite *pleasurable...* for me. And you're going to have a front row seat. You'll be begging me to kill her before the end."

The metal edge of the restraints dug into Isin's skin. He might not be able to use his hands, but he could still picture them wrapped around Kerr's throat, squeezing the life out of him.

Kerr shoved back with a smug smirk. "How's the hand?" He tapped on the tip of one of the needles.

Isin's body twitched involuntarily. A sensation cut through the fog, a subtle warning of impending pain. Not a good sign.

Kerr's brows lifted. "Felt that, did you? Good. The anesthesia is wearing off. In less than a minute, you'll be wishing you were dead."

Isin refused to look at his hand, but a slow burn building in his fingers indicated Kerr could be correct.

Kerr cocked his head, studying Isin with the focus of a cat watching a mouse. "I have one more task to accomplish before the pain blocks out everything else." He reached behind the med platform and brought out what looked like an old-fashioned boxing glove, except jointed pieces of metal had been attached to the front. The light flashed off the uneven surface as Kerr slipped the glove over his right hand. "I wouldn't want you to miss this."

Every swear word Isin knew bottled up at the back of his throat as he stared at Kerr. The glove was well padded. Kerr would be able to hit him without feeling a thing. But the metal on the outside could break bone.

"I owe you, traitor." Squaring off in a boxing stance, Kerr lashed out.

Isin had never taken a beating while strapped to a table. He couldn't avoid the assault, but he could minimize the damage. He moved his neck with the force of the blow, the metal cutting into the gap between his jaw and cheekbone.

He had time to draw a single breath before Kerr's fist connected again, striking perilously close to his eye and making it water. The third blow broke cartilage in his nose, sending rivulets of blood coursed over his lips and chin as pain radiated out in a starburst.

But he barely noticed. He was too busy tracking the fire ants that had started burrowing under the skin of his left hand. His fingers twitched of their own volition, igniting slivers of white-hot flame that wrapped around his fingers like a vise.

His teeth scraped together as his jaw clenched. A year of practice ignoring the messages from the pain receptors in his brain kept him from crying out, but his breath bellowed like a locomotive.

On some level he became dimly aware that Kerr had stopped punching him. Calling on the power of his own rage, he forced his eyes open and met Kerr's gaze.

Kerr was watched him expectantly, his lips moving and sound coming out, but Isin couldn't make sense of anything over the roaring in his ears.

Kerr's smile turned feral. He repeated the words more slowly. "How. Does. It. Feel?"

The needles had turned into red-hot pokers, lodged beside the bones in his fingers, pumping molten lava in a never-ending wave. He forced his lips to form one word on a pained exhale. "Great."

Kerr's harsh laugh filled the small room.

The screams from Isin's nerve endings had turned into a riot, tearing at his self-control. He didn't want to give Kerr the satisfaction of a reaction, but stellar light, it *buuurned.*

A small whimper might have escaped his lips, because Kerr's smile grew. "Don't worry, the effect of the drug will wear off in a few hours."

A few *hours!*

"Unless I give you another dose."

The primal snarl that clawed its way along Isin's throat promised a slow and painful death for his adversary. The tendons of his neck tightened as he fought to keep down the roar of pain building in his chest. He couldn't look at his hand, afraid he would see the skin melting away from the bone.

And then Kerr tapped the needles.

Isin's scream echoed in his ears, undulating in waves as Kerr repeated the tap.

Kerr's laughter joined in, a medley of sadistic horror. After Isin's cries faded away, replaced by the sawing of each inhalation, Kerr brought his face within a millimeter of Isin's ear. "So much better than I'd imagined."

Isin whipped his head to the side, his forehead connecting with Kerr's nose with a satisfying thump.

Kerr yelped, jerking back. His features contorted with fury. "You—"

"Kerr to the bridge." The tense female voice over the comm pulled Kerr's attention to the door.

His lips parted in a growl as he stalked over to the comm panel. "*I'm busy!*"

"A ship just entered the system."

"What kind of ship?"

"Unknown. They're still out of visual range."

Kerr's expression had switched from fury to annoyance. He glared at Isin like the interruption was somehow his fault. "I'll be right there."

Isin didn't take his gaze off Kerr as the lunatic approached the table. He pulled a slim case out of his pocket and opened it to reveal several auto-injectors filled with fluid. He selected one and pocketed the case, then placed the device against the vein at Isin's elbow and triggered the injector. "A little something extra while I'm gone."

What new hell had Kerr just unleashed in his system?

"When I return, we'll continue our... conversation." Kerr smacked Isin's left hand.

The blinding agony blocked out Kerr, the room, even the sound of his own shrieks. It wasn't until the wave crested and ebbed that he realized Kerr was gone.

Thirty-Three

Focus. Breathe. Focus.

Isin repeated the words as a lifeline to his sanity. The blistering lava field that was his left hand was far beyond any pain he'd faced before. But if he couldn't block it out enough to come up with an escape plan, it would only be the beginning.

With each breath, he analyzed one aspect of the room. It was all he could manage as tears streamed down his face. *Inhale. Door, closed. Exhale. Inhale. Comm panel, off. Exhale.*

Eventually his gaze reached the med platform, starting at his feet and working his way up. On breath five, he halted at the restraints holding his left arm. *Electronic panel, on.* It sat ten centimeters from his left hand. Three more focused breaths confirmed it operated the restraints. Could he reach it?

Clamping his jaw, he rotated his wrist to the left. The volcano that was his left hand erupted, ripping a cry from his lips.

Breathe. Breathe. Breathe!

The small part of his mind that still clung to rational thought shouted the warning. He was hyperventilating and would soon pass out.

No!

Fixing Kerr's face firmly in his mind's eye, he forced his attention back to his hand. Surprisingly, it was still attached to his arm, his fingers hovering two centimeters from the panel. Not close enough.

He slumped against the med platform but made certain his arm didn't move. *Two centimeters. And another one to reach the panel.* He could see the command for the release. It was positioned at the top of the panel. He just needed a three-centimeter tool that he could use to tap it.

His gaze shifted to his hand. *And the ability to grip a three-centimeter tool.*

That was the bigger problem. If rotating his wrist had triggered an explosion of pain, what would happen if he moved his fingers?

He looked to his right side. Maybe Kerr had left something within reach? He swiveled his shoulders to get a better look, sparking a blast that forced him back into hyperventilation alert mode.

When the danger passed, he took a good look at every millimeter within reach of his damaged right hand. Nothing. No tools, cables, wires, or random objects.

He eased onto his back and stared at the door. He had to get out before Kerr—

A tremor rocked the ship, knocking his arm against the restraints and wrenching a scream from his chest. Another tremor followed, jolting him in the opposite direction.

Sweat slicked his skin as he struggled to maintain consciousness.

Desperation set in, taking hold of his throat, choking him. He fought back, pouring all the pain and rage into a single-minded focus. He knew what he had to do.

A supernova went off in his hand as he brought it in contact with the material of his briefs. He screamed like a banshee, letting the pain flow through him as he caught the blunt end of the needle from his middle finger under the elastic circling his thigh. His cries filled the room in a continuous chain as he steadily pulled his hand away, working the needle out from underneath his skin.

His vision blurred but he kept going. When the needle slipped free, the agony downgraded, switching from supernova to solar flare.

He closed his eyes and sucked in air, the rasp of his breath the only sound in the room other than the dull thuds resounded through the hull. The med platform shook and the pain in his hand ratcheted up, but compared to what he'd just endured, it was a space walk.

Lifting his head, he spotted the needle, a shining metallic sliver against his dark skin, anchored by the elastic.

Grasping the sharp end of the needle between his ring finger and thumb produced a series of whimpers he didn't even try to contain. He might as well have been picking up a white-hot coal.

Lifting his wrist as high as the restraint would allow, he maneuvered his hand into position, the blunt end of the needle balanced over the control panel. The words *Restraint Release* swam in his vision, swaying back and forth like a ship on a rough sea. He swallowed around the bile rising in his throat before lowering the needle.

Boom!

The deck bucked, slamming his body into the restraints. An inferno ripped through his hand, sending shockwaves that left him gasping for air. His surroundings greyed out, his thoughts scattering like bolts tossed across the floor.

Time lost all meaning. Only the pain existed, stalking him like a predator, devouring him bite by bite.

When his senses finally returned, the first thing he heard was the rasp of air in his throat. Had he been screaming the entire time? Sweat made his skin as damp as his throat was dry.

His gaze zeroed in on his left hand. His *empty* left hand. The needle was gone.

He'd dropped it. The green tip lay on the deck near his pile of clothes.

His eyelids slid down, cutting out the glare of the lights, the only minor relief he could provide to his ravaged body. The med platform trembled as another jolt rocked the ship, smacking his hand against the restraint.

The sharp flash of pain galvanized him into action. His hand burned like he was holding it in a furnace, but a bubble of calm bobbed in the flow of molten lava coursing through his veins. He had one more chance. This time it wouldn't slip through his fingers.

Moving with deliberation, he brought his hand back to his briefs, hooking the second needle end under the elastic.

The torture of pulling the needle free tested his endurance, but having been through it once, he clung to the promise of relief that waited at the end of the inferno.

When the needle lay tethered to the elastic, he drew air into his lungs in huge gulps. With the needles no longer pressing on his skin and bones, the agony in his hand pushed back to a dull roar. But Kerr's chemical cocktail had done its job well. The slightest brush against his skin or movement of his fingers triggered a new shockwave of pain.

Picturing his enemy brought a surge of adrenaline. Gritting his teeth and releasing a feral growl, he grasped the needle's tip between his thumb and index finger. The growl turned into a howl as the contact sliced him like a blade.

Focus. Breathe. Focus.

One more chance at freedom. One more step. He could do this.

Blinking rapidly to clear the tears streaming from his eyes, he turned his wrist and maneuvered the blunt end of the needle into position, bringing it down on the panel.

Nothing.

He blinked again. The needle was too far to the right, not making contact with the release.

Adjusting the angle, he lowered the tip again.

A beep sounded from the panel and the restraints slid open.

He lurched away from the platform, stumbling and crashing to the deck as his legs failed to support his body. Self-preservation kept him from putting his hands out to catch himself, but the thump when he hit sent another bolt of lightning through his system.

He lay on the cold, pebbled surface, panting, his hands held aloft like a surgeon after scrubbing up. He glanced at the door, but it remained blissfully closed. For now. It wouldn't stay that way.

Using his elbows to lift his torso, he tucked his knees to his chest and rose to a crouch. The room swayed, but that had more to do with the vibrations shaking the ship than his equilibrium.

He'd accomplished his goal, but that still left him in a vulnerable position—stripped down, unarmed, and exhausted.

He flexed the fingers of his right hand and was rewarded with a screech of pain all the way to his shoulder. Broken bones in his wrist and hand from the feel of it. The pain wasn't an issue—compared to his left hand, it was a pin prick. But the muscles and tendons weren't responding to his commands, the swelling inhibiting movement.

Both of his hands were worse than useless.

He stared at his rifle lying on the deck. How was he supposed to get dressed, let alone hold and fire a weapon?

With great difficulty, it turned out.

He started with his pants, using his feet and crippled right hand to do the work of guiding them up to his hips. Securing them took way longer than it should have. He kept his gaze on the door, but Kerr didn't appear. Most likely he was still dealing with whatever ship was causing the deck to shimmy and shake.

Isin hadn't been able to concentrate on what the shaking had meant while he'd been strapped to the table, but his mind had cleared enough to fill in the blanks. Kerr's ship was under attack, most likely from someone he'd double-crossed—a long list. Unfortunately, that wasn't good news for either of them. If Kerr's ship was boarded or blown up, Isin would die with the crew. No one would stop to ask if he was friend or foe.

It also meant his crew was in danger on two fronts.

He searched the items on the floor, using his bare feet to lift and sort, but his comm device wasn't anywhere in the pile. The one thing he needed most, Kerr had taken. Or maybe it had been lost in the scuffle in the engine room.

He added a few more earthy epithets regarding Kerr's character to his growing collection while he evaluated the rest of the clothing. No point in trying to pull on his tunic. It would provide some protection, but sliding his hand through the tight sleeve... he didn't even want to imagine it.

Instead, he reached for his body armor, settling it across his torso and abdomen. The cool metal against his bare chest provided a soothing counterpoint to the heat in his hand. Securing it took creative thinking and flexibility, but he almost managed without incident. Almost. He hissed as the base of his palm brushed the metal, scorching his skin.

He called Kerr every nasty name he could think of as he swayed on his feet. But he stayed upright.

Kerr would pay for this. Oh, yes. He would pay.

His boots posed another challenge. He forced his feet into them without using his hands, but tightening them put his damaged right hand to the test. However, he didn't relish facing his enemy in bare feet, and loose boots would have been more of a hazard than protection.

Which left his weapons. Attaching his thigh holster one-handed took time, but leaving it wasn't an option. Not with the piece of shrapnel from the Setarip attack sewn into the lining. He needed that connection to Natasha now more than ever.

He hefted his rifle one-handed, slinging it over his shoulder and catching it under his right arm. He braced the rifle against his body and rested his finger on the trigger, testing the feel. He had enough strength and range of motion to squeeze the trigger, but not much else. If his targets cooperated by remaining still, he'd have a chance. If they moved, he'd be in trouble.

And if anything came in contact with his left hand...

He pushed the thought out of his mind. He couldn't waste energy thinking about the pain that awaited him outside the door. Cutting off the offending limb seemed like an excellent idea, but even if he wanted to, he couldn't—not with his right hand smashed up.

Kerr had said the effects would last a couple hours. How long since Kerr had left the infirmary? Thirty minutes? An hour? No way to know for sure. Just as he had no idea what he'd encounter on the other side of the door.

But that didn't change the situation. One way or another, he was getting off this ship.

Thirty-Four

He reached for the panel to open the door and paused, his hand throbbing with every beat of his heart.

Wait a minute. He was in an infirmary. Wasn't it logical he'd have access to anesthetics?

Stepping back, he shoved his rifle behind his hip so he could use his right hand to rummage in the infirmary's cabinets. Nothing on the shelves looked familiar.

Opening the drawers took more effort, his hand protesting the entire time, but his search produced a reward—a local anesthetic. He recognized the name from his various visits to Jake's infirmary. It probably wouldn't override the nerve drug Kerr had given him, but it might lessen the effect.

Positioning the injector took intense concentration, since the deck continued to shake unpredictably. But he succeeded in injecting the solution into his left wrist.

The seconds ticked by interminably as he waited. And waited.

A particularly hard jolt sent him stumbling against the counter. He caught himself with his right forearm, but his left hand followed his body's motion and brushed against his armor. Arrows of pain darted out, but nothing like the waves of lava he'd endured up to now.

Definitely an improvement. The anesthetic was working, although the appendage was still a serious liability. A direct blow could be crippling.

The tremors from the deck turned into quakes that challenged his balance as he headed back to the door. The battle outside had ramped up.

Positioning his rifle at his side, he took a steadying breath, mentally shifting into attack mode. He was likely to encounter at least two guards outside the door, and the only thing in his favor was the element of surprise. He'd have to make the most of it.

Bending his knees in a defensive crouch, he tapped the door panel. As soon as the opening was wide enough to fit through, he charged forward. And caught a lone guard flatfooted.

Before the guard could raise his weapon, Isin pivoted and fired. More by chance than skill, he caught the shorter man in the throat. That was the good news. But as the man staggered and fell, his return shot grazed Isin's left thigh.

The pain was familiar. The way it affected his balance was not. He stumbled toward the bulkhead, his left hand coming perilously close to taking the brunt of his weight as he instinctively reached out. A split second before making contact, he tucked his arm in, his shoulder and the side of his face smacking against the hard surface.

More pain as the jolt traveled down his arm to his hand. He pressed against the bulkhead, using it for balance as he turned his rifle toward the downed guard. But it was wasted effort. The man stared sightlessly overhead as blood pooled on the deck.

Isin drew in a shaky breath. First hurdle crossed. Only a thousand more to go.

He scanned the short passageway. No sign of movement, but now that he was out of the soundproofed infirmary, the cacophony of battle banged against his eardrums—resonant booms from the hull and the shriek of weapons fire in the passageways. Not that the chaos would help him. It might have covered the sounds of his dramatic exit, but as the guard had just proven, he was likely to get himself shot by anyone he encountered. He couldn't aim and he couldn't easily evade. He needed to stay hidden and keep moving.

The question was, which way? This section of the ship didn't look familiar, and unlike Sweep, he'd never been on a vessel like this one before. He couldn't even orient fore and aft so he could head back toward the airlock where he'd stowed his spacesuit.

He was lost.

A year ago, his situation would have paralyzed him. Not anymore. He'd trust his instincts to lead him.

He limped along the narrow corridor, passing storage lockers on both sides. The deck rose and fell under his feet, like a schooner caught in choppy water, making him list from side to side. He stopped, bracing his shoulder against the bulkhead.

The shifting stopped.

He straightened, and his surroundings started to move again.

Fantastic. The drugs were messing with his balance. Or more alarming, whatever Kerr had injected him with before leaving the infirmary was finally kicking in. Good thing he needed another challenge.

At the end of the corridor he came to a branched stairway.

Fifty-fifty chance. Up or down?

The shriek of nearby weapons fire from above paused that decision as he ducked into the shadows. He angled his rifle up, but aiming was futile without the full support of his hand. He was as likely to strike the stair treads as a target.

The blasts shifted direction, growing fainter.

He eyed the stairs, memories of another stairwell, another painful climb, seeping into his vision. This time he was determined not to pass out.

He leaned his forearm on the railing and placed his right leg on the first step, hauling his body up, step by step. Funny how something that a couple hours ago would have been effortless now took the strength of Hercules to accomplish.

The deck trembled, this time for real and not in his head. He leaned into the railing, fighting to stay on his feet. A tumble down the stairs would not help his situation.

A jolt tipped him sideways, his body weight dragging him to the edge of the step. He lunged forward, crashing onto the small landing three steps up and smacking both hands on the metal surface.

An explosion went off in his left hand while lasers cut into his right. He bit down on his lip to muffle the cry that erupted from his chest. Air scraped in and out of his lungs with each tortured breath.

Get up. Get up. Get up!

Peeling his eyelids open, he listened for sounds of movement on the deck above. The shrieks of weapons fire in the distance didn't seem to be heading his way.

Taking a deep breath, he pushed to his knees. He waited until the internal rocking stopped before rising to his feet and climbing the next set of stairs, reaching the upper deck with the speed of a snail.

Shouts and a burst of weapons fire brought him up short. He could barely keep his rifle from clanging against the railing, let alone aim and fire. He needed cover.

Stumbling in the opposite direction, he passed a tiny maintenance alcove to the left of the stairwell. It was little more than an opening between pipes and wires, but he shoved his shoulder into the gap, positioning his rifle facing out as he drew his left hand in close to his body.

The roar of weapons fire grew louder, the first blasts striking the bulkhead across from his hiding place. Footsteps pounded on the deck, heading right for him.

He held his breath and adjusted his finger on the trigger.

But the footsteps turned the corner and retreated down the stairwell he'd just climbed as more blasts struck the bulkheads.

After a moment the firing ceased, replaced by the whisper of voices in the passageway.

"...sign of him. We're following one down the stairwell."

The female voice was so unexpected, Isin froze. *Can't be.*

"Pete, cover me."

That confirmed it.

"Natasha!" Isin lurched out of his hiding spot, coming nose to nose with the business end of a rifle. Instinct made him pivot away, but his balance failed him, dropping him like a boulder onto the deck. Both hands struck the hard surface, shooting bullets along his nerve endings.

He rolled onto his back, panting.

"Isin?" Pete Stevens' voice.

He struggled to bring the images swimming before his eyes into focus. Someone crouched next to him, resting a warm hand on his bare shoulder.

"You look like hell." Stevens' face was lined with concern as he swept his gaze over Isin.

Movement behind him drew Isin's attention. A petite angel in a brown duster had appeared, a pistol in her hand and a frown pulling down the corners of her pale pink lips.

The frown turned into a thundercloud as she sank beside him. "What did that monster *do* to you?"

A rhetorical question, but he cherished the concern, and the promise of retribution, behind it.

She touched his left pant leg, pulling on the fabric and inspecting his wound. "You're losing blood." She dipped a hand into a pocket of her duster and produced a roll of stretch gauze.

He blinked. "You carry gauze?"

She met his gaze, a glimmer of humor behind the steel in her eyes. "I do when I'm around you."

He snorted, which came out sounding a little strange through his swollen nose. "Why didn't you tell me you were coming?"

"Because you would have told me not to."

Yes, he would have. And she would have ignored him anyway.

She wrapped the gauze around his leg with practiced efficiency. "That'll help." Her gaze darted down the passageway. "But we've got to get you out of here."

"Point the way." He'd follow her anywhere. And this time, he'd make sure she didn't put herself in unnecessary danger.

She and Stevens exchanged a glance. "What's the quickest route back?" she asked her engineer.

He tilted his head in the direction they'd come. "As long as we don't meet up with anybody."

Natasha touched her comband. "Itorye? We've got him."

"Is he all right?"

Natasha's gaze swept over him, lingering on his face. "He will be."

"We'll meet you at the airlock."

"On our way." She closed the channel. "Time to get up."

He flinched as she reached for his arm. "Watch my hands."

She glanced down. "Why?"

He lifted the right one. "Broken." Then the left. "Nerve damage."

Natasha's lips pressed together. "We'll be careful."

She and Stevens slid their arms under his torso and helped him to his feet. His left leg didn't think walking was a good idea. His right concurred. He staggered until Natasha caught him around the waist and gently eased his arm over her shoulder.

"Lean on me."

Déjà vu. Suddenly he was back on the dunes of Troi. He met her gaze. "I don't think—"

She picked up her cue, a tiny smile creasing her cheek. "Don't think. Walk."

They'd had the exact same exchange the day the Setarips had taken her from him. And here she was, saving him again. Apparently the universe believed he needed lessons in humility.

Stevens stayed several steps in front of them, rifle at the ready.

The deck shook under Isin's feet, and he stumbled into Natasha.

She grunted, but managed to keep them both upright even though he was twice her size. The woman had strength and balance to spare.

Another tremor, caused by what had to be a cannon blast, finally triggered a flash of the obvious. "Is that *Phoenix*?"

"Yep."

So Natasha's arrival had drawn Kerr out of the infirmary. Yet another debt he owed her.

They rounded a corner and came to a set of stairs. Stevens moved to Isin's other side, providing additional support as they started up.

Climbing was a lot harder than shuffling along the deck, even with their help. "How'd you... get... onboard?" he asked between steps.

"*Gypsy*. Itorye let us into *Vengeance*'s shuttle bay."

"Must have been... hard... evading fire from... Kerr's ship." *Gypsy* was an acrobatic shuttle in atmosphere, but far from a speed demon in the black.

Natasha and Stevens hesitated for a moment, another of those quick looks passing between them. A look that spoke volumes.

"What's wrong?" Tension wrapped around his neck. "Is *Gypsy* damaged?" Natasha loved that shuttle more than life. If it had been harmed during the flight in...

"*Gypsy*'s fine." Natasha glanced at him out of the corner of her eye, the muscles of her face tightening. "Sweep made sure of that."

"Sweep? Kerr didn't... capture him?" He hadn't dared to hope.

Natasha's expression darkened. "No. He didn't."

A cold knot settled into Isin's stomach. It wasn't what she'd said. It's what she hadn't said. He halted, tightening his grip on her shoulder until she met his gaze. "Where is he?"

The look in her eyes dragged an icy finger down his back. "He's dead."

Thirty-Five

Isin's mind rebelled against the words reverberating in his ears. *Sweep? Dead?* He didn't want to believe it. Sweep was indomitable. A rock. He couldn't die.

But he didn't see a shred of doubt in Natasha's pale eyes. "How?"

"Taking out the—" A blast shrieked past them, striking the back of the stairwell. Natasha shoved Isin against Stevens, slipping out from under his arm and bringing up her pistol. Two quick shots brought a scream of pain, a clatter, and a solid thump.

She kept her weapon up, scanning the open deck of what looked like a cargo hold at the top of the stairwell, but the space was empty. "All clear." She returned to Isin's side and they got him up the last few steps.

Sweep. Dead.

The two words echoed in his mind. With each repetition, they broke apart his initial shock like an ice floe at the equator, leaving behind a sea of boiling rage.

Kerr. He was responsible for this. *All* of this.

As Stevens scouted ahead, Isin limped alongside Natasha, painfully aware of the liability he posed. Normally he would have been the first to spot the shooter, and the quickest draw. In his present condition, he was useless. Worse than useless. What exactly was he going to do to protect Natasha from the next threat? Without his balance, he wasn't even an effective human shield.

Questions weighted down his tongue, but he didn't voice them. Distracting Natasha and Stevens would only put them at greater risk.

Stevens motioned them forward to an open hatch.

Isin didn't bother keeping track of his surroundings after that. Remaining upright required focus, as did keeping his left hand from brushing against his body, and making sure each shuffling step didn't take Natasha down.

To her credit, she didn't voice a single complaint. But a faint buzzing sound made her pause. She swiveled her wrist to glance at her comband before tapping the display. "What's wrong, Kenji?"

"We've got a problem. A ship—"

Green's screech overrode Kenji's explanation. "It's Rathburn! He's tracked me. We have to leave!"

Natasha's face pinched. "Kenji, what's she talking about?"

"A big ship entered the system. Green says—"

Green cut in again. "Rathburn's after the cube! You have to—"

"Kenji, shut her up!" Natasha looked like she was hanging onto her temper by a thread. "Is the ship a threat?"

"If it's gunning for us? Oh, yeah."

"Alert Itorye, then move *Phoenix* to a defensive position and await my orders. We're heading back to *Vengeance* now."

"You found Cap?"

"She... did," Isin ground out through clenched teeth. They weren't moving, but the passageway was still spinning.

Kenji's exhale came over the comm. "Good. That's good."

Isin grunted in response.

Natasha shot him a worried look, the line between her brows deepening. "I'll notify you when we're onboard."

"Got it."

Natasha closed the channel and started forward again. "Do you know what cube Green's talking about?"

"It's the... cargo we're... carrying." Speech had become a challenge.

"Where is it?"

"In my... cabin."

Natasha blew out a breath. "All right. That'll be our priority after we–"

"Get down!" Stevens shouted a nanosecond before a burst of weapons fire lit up the passageway.

Natasha pivoted to shield his body with her own, her arm tightening around his torso.

"No!" He resisted, but in his weakened state, she had more leverage.

She spun him behind a support beam before returning fire. "Is there another way to the airlock?" she shouted to Stevens over the roar of rifles.

"Not without crossin' half the ship," he shouted back from his position on the opposite side of the passageway.

Isin counted at least four different shooters, all out for blood. The stench of scorched metal filled the air as the blasts struck centimeters from his face. The supports were sturdy, but they weren't indestructible.

The fury of the blasts slowed.

"Hold your fire!" a male voice called out.

Isin stiffened. "Camp." Someone had let the traitor out of *Vengeance's* brig.

Natasha's brows lifted at his menacing growl. "Friend of yours?"

"Saboteur."

Her eyes narrowed, her gaze shifting back to the passageway. "What do you want, Camp?"

A couple beats passed. "That you, Summer?"

Summer? Natasha didn't sound anything like Summer.

Natasha smirked. "Strike one."

"Faraway?"

"Strike two."

"Willow?"

"Strike three. You're out."

"I don't care who you are. I just want Isin."

Natasha's jaw flexed. "Not gonna happen."

"Come on. He's not worth dying for."

Natasha's lips pulled back like a snarling she-wolf. "Wanna bet?"

Thirty-Six

Isin had no idea what he'd done to deserve Natasha's loyalty, but if the room hadn't been spinning, he might have kissed her.

Camp's voice went from cajoling to lethal. "If that's the way you want—"

A shot rang out, terminating Camp's threat. Isin risked a peek around the support beam.

Camp's body tumbled into the middle of the corridor, face-planting into the deck. A second shot clipped one of the remaining three shooters on the shoulder. She spewed obscenities, spinning around to fire behind her as another bolt knocked her to the ground, her weapon clattering to the deck and sliding away.

Stevens rose and fired, catching another man in the back.

The fourth shooter unleashed a barrage of shots in all directions.

Isin ducked as blasts struck the bulkhead.

The rifle fire ended abruptly, followed by a deathly quiet.

"That's better."

Isin recognized that voice, too. "Shash." She stood in the middle of the corridor, a rifle in one hand and an oversized handgun in the other.

He leaned on Natasha as he staggered out into the open.

"Itorye suggests you speed things up." The smirk on her face seemed to be directed at Natasha.

Natasha held her gaze. "Then let's go."

They reached the airlock connecting *Vengeance* to Kerr's ship without further incident. Isin drew in a deep breath as his boots touched *Vengeance*'s deck. He was home.

Itorye and Shorty were waiting for them, the screech of weapons fire echoing from the upper decks.

Itorye's gaze swept over Isin, but her expression didn't change. "The incoming ship will be in weapons range in seven minutes."

"Our... crew?" The words sounded unintelligible to his ears, but Itorye answered anyway.

"Needles and Downey are dead. Two of Kerr's teams are still onboard."

He turned to Shash. "Engines?"

She stopped glaring at Natasha and focused on him, shaking her head. "DOA."

His blood heated. Kerr had backed him into a no-win scenario. He wanted to find his nemesis and smash his body into pulp with his bare hands, then shoot him out an airlock and take *Vengeance* far, far away from this miserable system.

But his ship wasn't going anywhere. And he was in no condition to deal with Kerr, either.

Or the incoming ship. His instincts told him Green's pursuer meant business. If he wanted to salvage anything from this situation, he only had one option—abandon *Vengeance* and flee on *Phoenix*.

An ache lodged in his chest as he met Itorye's gaze. "Gather... the crew. To *Phoenix*."

She didn't comment, simply relayed his orders over the comm.

That just left the damn cube. There was no way he could climb the stairs to B deck. And now that Sweep was gone, Itorye and Shash were the only people who knew where the safe was located and how to access it.

"What about the cube?" Natasha murmured, as though she'd read his mind.

The shriek of weapons fire from the forward stairwell increased. His cabin was on the other side of that chaos. "My cabin. Help... Itorye."

Her gaze followed his to the stairwell. "Up there?"

He nodded.

A ghost of a smile crossed her lips. "You never make it easy, do you?"

At least one of them still had a sense of humor. "No." And he deeply regretted pulling her into his mess. Kerr would pay for that, too. "Be careful."

"Always." She turned to Shash. "Can you take him to Jake on the *Dagger*?" She slipped out from under his arm. "Don't touch his hands."

Shash grabbed him around the waist, not nearly as gentle as Natasha. But she kept him on his feet. "Where are you going?"

"I have a job to do." She leveled a look at Shash. "Keep him safe."

Isin opened his mouth to protest, but Shash beat him to it.

"We were doing just fine without you, little girl."

Natasha didn't even bother replying, just lifted her brows a fraction and turned away to confer with Itorye and Stevens.

Shash muttered what was most definitely not a compliment, then shot him a nervous look.

Ordinarily he would have given her a dressing down for maligning Natasha, but he couldn't summon the energy. Instead, he just stared until she looked away.

She put pressure on his ribcage to get him moving. "Shorty!" she barked. "Let's get him to the bay."

Shorty moved to his other side. As one of two members of the crew who stood taller than Isin, he helped Shash half-walk, half-carry him down the stairs to the shuttle bay.

Gypsy sat on the opposite side of the bay from the *Dagger.* Seeing the shuttle brought a strange sensation of calm. *Gypsy* had survived rough seas in the past. He trusted the sturdy vessel to get Natasha safely back to *Phoenix.*

Shash didn't seem to share his appreciation. She gave the shuttle a derisive sniff before pulling him toward the *Dagger.*

The ramp challenged Isin's balance as he climbed the incline. Shash and Shorty tightened their grip, practically lifting him off the ground. Summer greeted them at the top, still at her post. She stepped back so they could enter the transport.

The crewmembers already onboard stared at Isin as Shash and Shorty guided him through the main cabin, their expressions ranging from shock to mild curiosity. Most looked worse for wear themselves.

Jake met them in the tiny med area with medical scanner in hand. His eyes widened a fraction as he took in the image their trio made.

Great. If he was messed up enough to get an emotional reaction from Jake, he was even worse off than he thought.

"Kerr did something to his hands," Shash informed Jake as he lifted the scanner and ran it over Isin's body.

Jake focused on Isin's right hand. "Two fractured carpals, one fractured metacarpal." He shifted to the left one, a frown creasing his forehead. He checked the readings again before meeting Isin's gaze. "Did someone insert needles?"

Isin nodded. "Nerve... stimulator."

Ordinarily, Jake was an easygoing man. But there was nothing easygoing about the emotion driving a flush into his cheeks and a glint in his eyes. "Sadistic bastard," he muttered as he set the scanner down. "Let's see what's going on with the rest of you."

Shorty removed Isin's weapons and armor before helping him lie down on a collapsible med platform.

The horizontal position eased the dizziness, and the anesthetic he'd pumped into his wrist while on Kerr's ship had successfully neutralized the worst of the burning in his left hand.

Byrd lay on a matching platform to his right, a white sheet covering his body to his chest, angry red burn marks visible on his face and hands. His eyes opened as Shorty and Shash stepped aside. "Captain?" The name came out as a question, as though he wasn't certain he'd correctly identified Isin.

"Byrd."

Jake stepped between them, positioning the scanner in front of Isin's face. The frown lines around his mouth and eyes deepened. "What did he hit you with?"

"Metal... glove."

"I see." Jake packed a cargo bay's worth of meaning into those two words. He knew Kerr well enough to envision the scenario.

Isin allowed his eyes to drift closed as Jake continued his assessment. They'd been in this scenario more times than he could count, although usually because he'd volunteered for a Cage match, or purposely prolonged a fight with an enemy to push his limits for endurance and pain. It might have been his imagination, but Jake's touch seemed even gentler than normal.

The rapid staccato of boot heels on the deck and the whine of the exterior hatch sealing brought him out of his musings. He opened his eyes to find Itorye at the foot of the platform.

She had a bulky storage pack over one shoulder that looked filled to capacity. She gave him a subtle nod.

She had the cube.

"The bay's sealed. Orlov and Stevens are powering up *Gypsy*. All other crew are accounted for. Kerr's ship has disengaged from the airlock, but they're having trouble releasing the grappling lines."

So Kerr was attempting to flee from the incoming ship, too. He wasn't a total idiot. But he'd been caught in his own snare.

"Follow Natasha... out." He wanted to make sure she got away safely. They'd leave Kerr to deal with their uninvited guest.

"Aye." Itorye headed for the cockpit.

Jake took her place, resting his hands on the edge of the platform. "I'm getting abnormal blood readings. Did Kerr inject you with anything besides the nerve agent?"

A little something extra while I'm gone.

"Yes."

"What was it?"

"He... didn't say."

Jake drew in a slow breath. "Okay. I'll start analyzing."

A low-level hum came up through the platform as the *Dagger*'s engines warmed up. The voices of the crew drifted back to him, subdued and angry.

He'd never envisioned a scenario where he'd be forced to abandon ship. *Vengeance* was supposed to be an impregnable fortress.

The vibration from the deck intensified as the engines gained power.

"She's not what I expected."

Isin glanced at where Jake was setting up an IV drip. "Who?"

"Natasha. From your stories, I pictured someone... larger."

Isin grunted. Only a child would view Natasha as large. "You... met her?"

"I gave her the med supplies she was carrying."

Of course. That explained the gauze.

"But I can see why you like her."

Like her? That didn't come close to explaining the emotions Natasha inspired. "She saved... my life."

"I know. And she came here to do it again. She obviously believes it's a life worth saving."

She'd confirmed that when Camp had challenged her. What he couldn't figure out was why.

Jake inserted the IV, then fitted Isin's right hand with a healing cast.

Itorye's voice came over the ship's comm. "Opening bay doors." A shudder passed through the transport, indicating they'd lifted off.

And he was lying on a med platform.

An image of Natasha flying *Gypsy* out of the shuttle bay and coming nose to nose with the incoming ship jerked him upright.

"Whoa!" Jake put a restraining hand on his shoulder. "What are you doing?"

The room spun, reminding him that vertical wasn't a good position right now. Too bad. "Have to get... to the... cockpit." Preferably without passing out.

Jake's grip tightened. "Itorye can handle it."

Isin shook him off with a growl, levering his legs over the side of the platform and sliding until his boots touched the deck. He promptly collapsed, falling against the platform, barely halting his momentum with his forearms before his knees hit the ground.

Jake took hold of his upper arm. "Stubborn fool." But instead of trying to pull him back, he helped him up, slipping one arm around Isin's waist and grabbing the IV with his other hand. "Let's go."

With Jake's support, they made the lurching journey through the ship to the cockpit.

Itorye didn't even glance at them when they appeared behind her. "I wondered when you'd get here."

Shash sat in the copilot's seat, the weapons display visible over her shoulder. That left only the jump seat available.

Jake eased Isin onto it, hooking the IV on one of the upper storage compartment knobs. "I'll be right back."

Isin barely heard him. His focus was on the viewport. The bay doors had already parted, revealing the inky starscape. *Gypsy* sank out of sight.

Itorye guided the *Dagger* through the opening, following Natasha. The view shifted as they passed along the wide channel under *Vengeance's* belly, the stars beckoning from up ahead and below.

Isin stared at the aft camera view, which gave him a clear image of *Vengeance* as they emerged into open space. The dull ache lodging in his chest gave him new respect for how Natasha must have felt when she'd been forced to leave *Gypsy* behind after they'd crash-landed on Troi.

At the time, he hadn't even considered her feelings. All he'd been thinking about was saving himself.

"Flight pattern Maple Leaf. Kenji take point."

Natasha's voice over the comm drove the ache deeper. She was in danger now because of him, and he was as helpless to save her as he had been on Troi. Kerr was right. He deserved to suffer and die.

Gypsy shot away to port. He lost visual as Itorye banked the *Dagger* in the opposite direction, streaking off to starboard.

Jake returned, but Isin kept his focus on the viewport. "Where's... *Phoenix?*"

Shash pointed at the blue icon on the display traveling at a forty-five degree angle to their trajectory. Kerr's ship, shown in orange, was farther to port, accelerating away from *Vengeance.* The incoming ship's icon was highlighted in red, and closing fast on Kerr's ship.

"*Gypsy?*"

Shash indicated a second blue icon, this one traveling in the space between Kerr's ship and *Phoenix.* Even with his vision swimming, the display made it easy to see the shuttle was moving a lot slower than the rest of the ships in the field. And it was the only one without an interstellar drive. His argument with Natasha when they'd attempted to outrun the Setarips at Troi replayed in his mind. *Gypsy* was fast in atmo. Not in the black.

Unfortunately, the only nearby planet was the gas giant, and *Gypsy*'s shields couldn't withstand the pressure or radiation of the atmosphere. The shuttle would be crushed in seconds. Until Natasha could dock with *Phoenix,* she had nowhere to go.

Even worse, the *Dagger* was heading in the opposite direction. "Have to... defend *Gypsy.*"

Itorye glanced at him. "This was her plan. Scatter the ships so our new arrival has to choose who to follow."

"But she's—"

"The only one not carrying valuable cargo." Itorye leveled him with a look.

A look that said he wasn't thinking like a captain.

He glanced at the display. The layout of ships put *Phoenix* and the *Dagger* furthest from the incoming vessel. His transport carried the cube. *Phoenix* had Green. They needed both if they wanted to get paid. But Natasha was... expendable.

His teeth ground together. No, she wasn't. Never that. Forget that she'd saved his life. Again. She mattered because she was... Natasha. He had to—

"Kerr's ship just got hit with some kind of energy weapon." Data streamed across Shash's display. "It took out shields, engines, everything except life support. They're drifting."

Isin's vision blurred, making the images unreadable. He squinted, struggling to bring it back into focus.

"The enemy ship has altered course, moving to intercept *Gypsy.*"

No.

"She's countered. Trajectory at one-hundred-eighty to *Phoenix.*"

Baiting the other ship, leading it away, just as she'd led the Setarips away from his hiding place on Troi.

Help her! A garbled grunt erupted from Isin's chest as he shoved to his feet. Or tried to.

"Stop!" Jake grabbed him as his legs buckled, squeezing him in a bear hug to keep them both from hitting the deck.

The bridge spun, light and color dancing in front of his eyes without cohesion.

"They're firing at the shuttle." Shash's voice, muffled, like he had cotton stuffed in his ears.

Natasha.

"Missed. She's changing course again."

He blinked rapidly, desperate to bring the tactical display into focus.

Natasha's voice came over the comm. "Get to the jump windows. Pete and I will keep our guests busy."

No! Not again! But he couldn't get the words through his lips. Weights pressed down on his tongue and pushed his eyelids closed.

"You have to lie down," Jake ordered. "Movement stimulates the toxin."

Have to fight. Natasha...

"Good luck." Itorye's voice.

"You, too."

Natasha's words reverberated in his mind as he fell into a pool of nothingness.

Thirty-Seven

"...be fine, but not if he doesn't rest."

The male voice drifted through Isin's consciousness like the tendrils of a forgotten dream. The next voice was clearer.

"That's not Cap's way."

Kenji?

"Better than passing out. He'll have to choose."

Jake, speaking in his *I'm dealing with a difficult patient* voice. He'd used that tone every time Isin had been brought into the infirmary.

Isin pried his eyes open. Dim lighting. And a room he didn't recognize.

Jake, Kenji, and Itorye stood in a loose semi-circle near the foot of the med platform.

Itorye glanced at him, noting with a lift of one thin brow that he was awake. "He'll rest. I'll see to it."

So they'd been discussing him. "Meaning what exactly?" At least, that's what he tried to say. It came out as a scratchy rasp of air along his dry throat.

Jake looked his way, then walked to the counter and fetched a thimble-sized cup of water. "Sip this."

He took the offering, downing it in one swallow. He held it out for a refill, but Jake shook his head. "Moderation."

He glared, for all the good it did. Instead, he shifted his attention back to Itorye. "Meaning what?" he repeated.

"You need to take it easy. Jake had to work some magic to rid your body of whatever toxic soup Kerr pumped into you."

The cobwebs cleared, images of Kerr's attack, the torture in the infirmary, and the rescue flooding him in a tidal wave.

Natasha!

He lurched upright, but Jake clamped his hands on his right shoulder, Kenji grabbed his left shoulder, and Itorye planted herself right in front of him.

"Lie back down." Itorye spoke with the authority of a parent talking to a disobedient child.

"Natasha—"

"We can't help her."

"But—"

"At least, not right now." Itorye took a step closer as Kenji and Jake applied pressure to his shoulders. "But we *can* help you. Lie down."

His mind rebelled, but his body was all in favor of obeying Itorye's command. While Jake repositioned the platform so he could sit up, Kenji added a few plush pillows behind his back. Which clued him in to where he was. "We're on *Phoenix.*"

"That's right." Itorye sat on the edge of the platform. "After our initial jump, Kenji and I met at our pre-arranged rendezvous point and linked the ships together. We've been in an interstellar jump ever since."

He glanced between them. "Who's at the helm?"

"Byrd."

So the pilot had recovered enough from his burns to return to his job. But he wasn't the person who should be up on the bridge. "Natasha—"

"Ordered us to leave. She had that right. This was her command, remember?"

How could he forget? His gaze swept the infirmary. "Where's Green?"

"On B deck with the cube. Shash is keeping an eye on her."

"Did you find out what's in the cube?"

"She's refusing to tell us."

A growl rumbled in his chest. "She'll tell me." He flexed the fingers of his left hand, relieved when the motion didn't produce any burning or pain. His right hand was out of the healing cast Jake had placed on it while they were on the *Dagger*. His wrist was still stiff, but no longer swollen. He touched his face, running his fingers over his nose and around his eye. Both were tender to the touch.

Jake joined Itorye at the foot of the bed. "I went ahead and repaired the previous damage to the cartilage in your nose when I reset it. I used the image I had on file from your initial physical to put it back to the way it looked before you started offering up your face as a punching bag in the Cage."

Isin traced the scar on his cheek. Jake hadn't removed that, thank goodness. He'd fought hard to earn that mark, and to keep it. "How long have I been out?"

"Three hours."

Three hours. An eternity. Anything could have happened to Natasha in that time. And for all he knew, they were moving further away from her with every passing minute.

"How soon can I leave the infirmary?"

"Twelve hours."

Like hell. "Try again."

Jake's mouth tightened. "Eight hours."

"Two."

"Isin—"

"Don't argue, Jake." His tone came out sharper than he'd intended, but his emotions were raw. This day was now running neck and neck with the worst day of his life—the day Natasha had been taken by the Setarips. "Sweep is dead. We abandoned *Vengeance* and Natasha. I want answers from Green about her mysterious cube, and I want them now."

A flash of concern crossed Itorye's face as she stood. "What do you plan to do?"

Heat radiated through his chest, rising along his neck to his temples. He spoke with deliberation. "Either she'll tell me what's inside that cube and why this Rathburn person wants it so badly, or I'll find out how long she can breathe in space."

Natasha Orlov leaps out of the frying pan and into the firefight in RESURGENT RENEGADES, book three in the Starhawke Rogue trilogy.

Nat fired the port side thrusters. An energy blast streaked past meters from the shuttle's flank before continuing into the void. "Good thing we're tiny," she muttered. The narrow beam of the ship's weapon was clearly calibrated to take on large targets, not shuttles.

She pulled *Gypsy* up toward Kerr's ship, avoiding another blast that raced toward them.

Kenji's voice boomed over the comm. "Nat, I'm coming to get you."

"Don't you dare!" She glared, even though Kenji couldn't see her. "Get Green and *Phoenix* out of the system."

"We can't leave you."

"Yes, you can." She appreciated his loyalty, but right now, it was misplaced. "This Rathburn person wants two things—Green and whatever's in that cube. If he catches you, we're sunk. You get to that jump window and keep running until you can rendezvous with Itorye and Isin."

"But—"

"Stop arguing. Go!"

Dread filled the two syllables of Kenji's reply. "Aye, Cap."

She made a quick check of the status monitor to confirm *Phoenix* was still heading out of the system. Yep.

Twin blasts lanced out from the ship at a crisscross diagonal. She evaded one, but the second nipped *Gypsy*'s starboard wing. The cockpit lights flickered.

"Starboard engine's goin'," Pete said.

She eased up on the port engine to keep the shuttle from spinning, gliding past the belly of Kerr's ship. She fired the braking thrusters to slow their momentum, using the drifting vessel as a barrier between her shuttle and the metal predator stalking them.

The reprieve wouldn't last long. She was a mouse evading a cat by hiding under a fallen leaf. Eventually it would dig its claws into her.

But she'd take every second she could get. It would buy Kenji and Itorye time to get *Phoenix* and the *Dagger* out of the system.

If Isin had been in control of either vessel, her order would have fallen on deaf ears. He would have turned back to help her—logic and good judgment be damned. But thanks to Kerr, Isin was so banged up he wasn't in a position to save anyone, including himself. And Itorye wasn't the type to let emotions get in the way of practicality. She'd promised Nat that she'd get him away safely. She'd keep her word.

Isin would pitch a fit when he found out, even while lying half-comatose on a med platform. Too bad. They'd already lost *Vengeance* because of Kerr's treachery. She wasn't about to let the new arrival take out *Phoenix*.

She glanced at Pete. "Any ideas?"

He ran a hand along his unruly beard. "Tell 'em we're tourists?"

She barked out a laugh. Count on Pete to take their predicament in stride. "Think they'd believe that?"

A small smile curved his lips. "Could be. You're the best storyteller I know."

Storyteller. Not liar. Although truth be told, she was both.

Gypsy's running lights reflected off the gunmetal grey hull of Kerr's ship as the shuttle crept forward. Kerr was up there somewhere. With any luck, he'd been injured in the mad dash to escape the cruiser. She'd only been face-to-face with him once, but it had been enough to convince her he was the scum of the universe.

Pete checked the status monitor. "The *Dagger* just left the system."

"And *Phoenix*?"

"Almost... yeah, they're gone, too."

Nat exhaled on a weary sigh. For better or worse, they were on their own.

Captain's Log

The making of a mercenary

When Elhadj Isin (pronounced EYE-sin) appeared in ROGUE, the prequel where he and Nat encountered the Setarips on Troi, I had no idea that one day he would become a mercenary and captain of his own ship. In fact, I didn't expect to ever see him again. But when Nat decided to return to Troi and claim *Phoenix*, she triggered a sandstorm of questions about his fate, questions I had to answer.

Who was Isin? Where had he come from? How did he end up working with smugglers? And how did Nat's selfless act to save his life change him?

Answering those questions led to this story. Delving into his background provided some fascinating insights into his character, his family history, and the man he chose to become after losing Nat.

The prominent scar on his face also became an important element, the outward symbol of his internal struggle and his desire to be reminded every time he looked in the mirror of his failure to protect Natasha. It went through several iterations as the story unfolded. In the beginning I described it as smaller and located above his lip, but as I worked with my cover designer, we played with different versions until she came up with the image that graces the cover of this book. Suddenly I was looking into Isin's eyes, completely captured by my vision coming to life.

Every hero needs a villain

As I developed Isin's backstory, another character rose to the surface — Kerr. Initially, he came across as a poorly educated, bad-tempered malcontent, but I quickly realized Isin needed a nemesis whose mental abilities more closely matched his own. Rather than a street brawl, these two were entwined in an elaborate spy game, each trying to outwit the other.

Kerr's hatred for Isin came through loud and clear from the moment he appeared on the page, but I didn't discover the full extent of his loathing until Isin ended up strapped to the med platform, completely at Kerr's mercy. That scene practically wrote itself, Kerr taking me through his chilling plans with cool efficiency.

Gallows Edge

I first wrote about this outpost in THE HONOR OF DECEIT, book three in the Starhawke Rising series, when Nat and Aurora Hawke meet in Doohan's bar. Returning to it in this book was great fun, especially seeing it through Isin's perspective, since he had very little knowledge about Nat's life while she'd been a captive of the Setarips. It gave me great satisfaction to watch her sitting at the bar, enjoying a beer, without worrying that the collar around her neck would kill her if she stepped out of line, or that Tnaryt would punish her if she failed to bring back new recruits for the Setarips to torment. Having her win the bet with Isin made the moment even sweeter!

The crew of Vengeance

Populating Isin's ship full of mercenaries was a delightful challenge, especially naming the characters. I started with Itorye (eye-TORE-e), Kenji (Ken-gee), Sweep, and Byrd, drawing inspiration from people I worked with for two summers at a Girl Scout camp. We had a lot of wonderful adventures living in the pines, which fit the feel I wanted for this crew, so I ended up making all the names of the crew relate in some way to people or places from those memorable and fun summer days.

What's in the cube?

Pick up a copy of RESURGENT RENEGADES and find out!

Enjoy the journey!
Audrey

P.S. I always write to music, so if you'd like to experience this story the way that I did, listen to the film score for *Pirates of the Caribbean: Dead Man's Chest* while you read.

Audrey Sharpe grew up believing in the Force and dreaming of becoming captain of the Enterprise. She's still working out the logistics of moving objects with her mind, but writing science fiction provides a pretty good alternative. When she's not off exploring the galaxy with Aurora and her crew, she lives in the Sonoran Desert, where she has an excellent view of the stars.

For more information about Audrey and the Starhawke universe, visit her website and join the crew!

AudreySharpe.com

www.ingramcontent.com/pod-product-compliance
Lightning Source LLC
Chambersburg PA
CBHW050404190726
48284CB00007BB/2428